MW00623543

Primo DeLuca

Savage Bloodline Series

Mafia Romance

By:

Keta Kendric

Primo DeLuca

Copyright © 2022 by Keta Kendric

All rights reserved. No part of this publication may be reproduced, distributed or transmitted in any form or by any means, without prior written permission of the publisher and author, except for the use of brief quotations in a book review.

This is a work of fiction. Names, characters, places, and incidents are a product of the author's imagination. Locales and public names are sometimes used for atmospheric purposes. Any resemblance to actual people, living or dead, or to businesses, companies, events, institutions, or locales is completely coincidental.

Cover: Cosmic Letterz

Editing: A. L Barron, One Last Glance Editing

ISBN: 978-1-956650-05-1/Primo DeLuca

Contents

CHAPTER ONE	9
CHAPTER TWO	17
CHAPTER THREE	23
CHAPTER FOUR	35
CHAPTER FIVE	41
CHAPTER SIX	65
CHAPTER SEVEN	79
CHAPTER EIGHT	93
CHAPTER NINE	99
CHAPTER TEN	107
CHAPTER ELEVEN	113
CHAPTER TWELVE	123
CHAPTER THIRTEEN	137
CHAPTER FOURTEEN	143
CHAPTER FIFTEEN	151
CHAPTER SIXTEEN	165
CHAPTER SEVENTEEN	171
CHAPTER EIGHTEEN	183
CHAPTER NINETEEN	193
CHAPTER TWENTY	199
CHAPTER TWENTY-ONE	211
CHAPTER TWENTY-TWO	235
CHAPTER TWENTY-THREE	243
CHAPTER TWENTY-FOUR	251
CHAPTER TWENTY-FIVE	261
EPILOGUE	273
OTHER TITLES BY KETA KENDRIC	281
CONNECT ON SOCIAL MEDIA	287

Synopsis:

Nevah: A night out with my girlfriends flipped my boring life on its head, and I ended up in the hands of a sexy mob boss who was the living manifestation of danger. The only fix to the problem I stepped into left me anchored to Primo DeLuca, who declared we were in a relationship before he even knew my name.

Primo: The last thing you're supposed to do when murder and mayhem are nipping at your back, is take on a relationship. But I'd never been one to take the easy way out of a situation. With bullets flying, bodies dropping, and murderous schemes unfolding all around us, I was ready to torment the devil and run hell before I let anyone take Nevah away from me.

Warning: This book is a multicultural romance that contains explicit language, graphic violence, and strong sexual content. It is intended for adults.

Chapter One

Primo

A deep refreshing inhale relieved my lungs but did nothing to release the muscles clenched with biting tension in my neck and back. Sleep beckoned, but I ignored the silent call to answer a more primal urge, one that called for an order of death with a side dish of devastation.

Upholding my Caporegime (Capo) position and ensuring our family duties were met was paramount to my region in St. Louis. My reign as Capo for the past two years had gone smoothly, only requiring me to bring out the brutal savage that resided within me a few times. However, trouble greeted me upon my return from Sicily, where I attended Don Ermanno's funeral and the crowning of Don Enzo, the new head of our family.

The emotional and criminal fallout of Don Ermanno DeLuca's recent death stirred up trouble within the family as well as with our enemies. There was always an adversary willing to risk it all to test a DeLuca, and we were a very accommodating family.

Two days after my return, I didn't resume my normal duties, but played the role of a detective who was attempting to learn why two of my men had dropped bodies. A failed hit was executed against them while they made a routine drop.

As expected, other families and crime syndicates assumed we were vulnerable and easily distracted due to our late Don's death. They were going to take their opportunities to strike, unaware that the DeLuca bloodline could process several emotions in the same breath.

Pain, anger, fear, and sorrow were the emotions experienced by most. DeLucas created another emotion—savage. We could mourn the loss of our Don, celebrate a new one, and put a bullet in a motherfucker's head for testing us all while letting tears fall.

Another deep inhale lifted my chest high, the oxygen feeding my brain before I released a long sigh. I could count on one hand how many hours of sleep I'd had in the past three days, but day-to-day operations were an all-consuming entity that didn't understand the body's physical limitations.

Today, the sun had risen and laid a new source of trouble at our doorstep. A robbery attempt at one of our stash houses left one of my men dead. My last three hours were spent processing the scene and determining that the break-in wasn't a run-of-the-mill robbery.

No evidence of a struggle was found, nor were any of the doors damaged, indicating the culprit was more than likely invited into the house. One of my most loyal men, Geno, was shot, execution-style, in the back of the head. The reinforced steel door securing the money room hadn't been touched. All that was taken from the premises was his phone and computer equipment, which indicated it was a fact-finding mission—someone gathering information on my family.

This drive tonight was the closest I would get to a break, so I concentrated on the powerful growl of my black Charger's Hellcat supercharged V8 engine. When too many thoughts clogged my head, I turned them off and focused on one mundane function.

My phone rang, a sound that was about as devastating as being shot in the ass. The disturbance caused dread to creep into my brain, putting an end to my mental respite and reopening my mind's freeway.

"Yes," I grumbled.

"Primo. I hope you're on the way. Shit is getting crazy enough to make my trigger finger itch."

It was my cousin, Brizio, whose club I was currently driving towards for an emergency meeting.

"Leandra's here, crying and shit. Said two guys just tried to grab her. She made it to her SUV and got away, but they shot at her. Took out her rear window."

"Motherfuck!"

My fist pounded into the steering wheel making the horn honk loudly from the angry punch I threw.

"My sentiments exactly," Brizio agreed, the irritation in his tone coming across the phone line.

"I'll be there in about ten minutes."

"Okay. See you then."

He clicked off.

A scowl sat like a prominent fixture on my face, the ache of my anger causing it to deepen. A fucking future dead body had my name stamped on it for attempting to take out multiple members of this family with no rhyme or reason to their actions.

My car engine responded with a loud roar when I slammed my foot down on the gas. I zoomed past other motorists, the swirl of colors from head and taillights swiping past my tunneling vision. This must have been what my thoughts coursing through my brain resembled.

A flash of light peeked into my peripheral vision, causing me to whip my head around in time to meet the blinding glare of a vehicle's rapidly approaching headlights. The shine put serious stress on my corneas, making me squeeze my eyes shut for a second.

The front bumper of a black Dodge Ram was at my rear passenger side, so close the driver could have puckered up to kiss my bumper's shiny ass cheek. On guard now, I reached for one of my peacemakers, a stainless steel FNX .45.

The impact of the first metal-clapping bump was slight, a tap. However, at seventy-five miles per hour, a tap was all that was required to encourage momentum, force, and gravity to send me into a spin.

My car rejected the turn I forced on it with my aggressive maneuvering. The tires left burned rubber on the highway and protested with a loud, car-shaking scream at my attempts to steer into the spin.

A concrete divider sat immovable on my side of the highway, and motorists speeding along in the lane on the passenger side had no idea that two tons of revved-up metal were aiming to get at them. A spin-out would cause a deadly crash or a possible pile-up.

My hands worked, frantic and fast, weaving into the only open space on the highway to keep from hitting other motorists. The black truck didn't abandon its aggressive attack. It delivered a harsher bump this time, forcing my Charger to slide over the road like the zipper of a horny teen's jeans.

When my car lost its fight with the relentless force of momentum, the crushing impact of my front bumper striking a gray SUV snapped my neck with a harsh jerk to the left. The side of my head struck the window and bounced off of it like a pin after a bowling ball strike. A concussion was a strong possibility based on the way pain detonated in my head and shot down my body like lightning before pulsing back up to my skull.

My car came to an abrupt metal-crunching stop, the passenger side slamming into a strip of guardrail. The thick line of silver metal burst through the passenger side window and pushed through the door before it rested in my passenger seat. I would have been a glob of pulverized meat if the impact had occurred on the driver's side.

The scent of burned rubber and engine exhaust perfumed the air, thick and suffocating. Raw anger coursed through my veins and pushed vengeance-seeking adrenaline through me. The strength of the emotion automatically snapped me into savage mode.

I blinked through blurred vision and my body ached like a motherfucker, but it didn't stop me from moving with purpose and determination, snatching my door handle, and kicking it open.

Using the door for cover, I jumped out of the car and aimed in every direction until I found the assholes who ran me off the road. My vision zoomed in and out of focus.

Was it more than one person? Who were they? What did they want?

"Pré...mo! De...Lu...ca!"

They sounded out every syllable of my name so that there was no mistaking who they addressed. The booming voice I believe came from a loudspeaker met my ears.

"The Malizioso is coming. See you soon!"

The deafening screech of their tires added to the pounding in my head. The black, darkly tinted truck jetted off like an evil streak of death, leaving me aching to put a fucking bullet in someone's skull.

The Malizioso were at the top of the food chain in the contract killing arena. Their reputation spoke of skills so deadly the group was known to provide their target a warning, making them aware that they were in their cross-hairs before they started the official hunt.

The notorious group wanted their targets prepared for a fight so that the hunt would be a much more deadly game. Their hitmen and women planned their kills months in advance and were given budgets to accomplish their missions.

In my line of work, I was imprisoned before, tortured, stabbed, and shot, but this was my first time landing on an official hit list. At thirty-eight, I had lived about a decade longer than was expected. Being the family hitman for nineteen years and running, I recently added Capo of St. Louis to my resume.

Now that Don Ermanno was gone, we expected other families to flex their muscles and test us but targeting *me* was making a whole other statement. They wanted this smoke, they damn well better expect the fires of hell to come with it.

I spat out a wad of blood and swiped more from my lip while staring after the taillights of the truck that hit me.

"Sir, are you alright?" a concerned Good Samaritan asked.

Several cars had stopped to help, but I didn't acknowledge a broader glimpse of my surroundings until the red I was seeing had cleared and my temperature cooled to that of a human

Now that my blood was no longer boiling an unusually cool breeze for July whispered along my skin. It provided an ominous touch that hinted at the trouble on the horizon.

This scene, the people's stressed faces, their anxious movements, and concerned voices was no longer white noise. The driver of the vehicle I hit was out and standing, and a woman who stopped to help wiped blood from his forehead.

I lifted my phone to my ear.

"I'm going to be late."

I growled the words and clicked off, not in the mood to explain shit over the phone. The sound of sirens in the distance drew closer. My phone was up to my ear again after I hit one of eight numbers that made up my speed dial list.

"Come to the city. I'm a target. The Malizioso," was all I said before hanging up.

Chapter Two

Primo

The vibe of the club scene turned my stomach, and I had a strong one. The sight of multiple men and women soliciting sex, the drink buying rituals, and the public displays of foreplay were for the insecure.

The world was filled with infinite choices and hanging your hopes on finding something worthwhile inside a club was a fucking joke you were playing on yourself. I didn't have time for the games, tiptoeing around feelings, and role-playing. I blurted my request and demands, and if the woman couldn't get with it, I moved the hell on, ego unaffected.

Regardless of my opinion about the club, it was where some of the most important DeLuca meetings took place. My cousin, Brizio's club, Hard Rain, was a premier spot in downtown St. Louis. It was a place to dance and have drinks, eat some of the best toasted ravioli in the city, and enjoy an impressive architectural display that rivaled that of the Cathedral Basilica of Saint Louis. The club was not only praised by local celebs, but it was also a quick and painless way of distributing a large percentage of our product.

I worked my way up the organizational hierarchy and sat in what I liked to call a middle management position. My responsibilities included safeguarding the lives of hundreds of men as well as millions of dollars from our business ventures.

Drugs, gambling, prostitution, and theft were among the products and services we offered. Construction and real estate were the foundations in which most of our ventures were built.

I lingered in the darkness clinging to the tight alley along the side of Hard Rain. I instructed my cousin Umberto, who I'd called to pick me up, drop me off here. My eyes roamed, scanning my surroundings with sharp eagle-eyed precision before stepping out and marching to the front of the line waiting for entry.

The guards manning the front doors made eye contact with me at my approach. One removed the metal chain they used as a minor barrier to keep out unwanted guests. The other gave me a two-fingered salute and a nod before I moved past him to step through the thick hardwood doors.

The music slapped me in the face the moment I stepped inside. Noise. Hot bodies, moving and gyrating. Drunken shouts, slurred speaking, and groping. My throat tightened when I inhaled a whiff of that *desperate-for-sex* scent permeating the air.

Fuck, I hated clubs.

"Primo DeLuca," a delicate female voice purred and somehow managed to project over the music. I turned to find Leandra DeLuca, the wife of the former Capo of St. Louis, my cousin Emmanuelle DeLuca. Even though he'd been dead for two years now, we respected Leandra because she was known for putting in work on the family's behalf, solidifying her loyalty and worth.

"Leandra." I offered her a nod and forced a smile.

She reached up to touch my face, but I wasn't having that shit. I drew back, flashing her a severe side eye in warning.

The woman's persistence amazed me. She smoothly ignored my warning, went up on her toes, and landed a kiss on my cheek. I endured Leandra's unwanted advances out of respect and always did my best not to lead her on in any way.

This dance of unreciprocated attentiveness had been ongoing between us for years. I was just not interested. I gave her credit for being a beautiful woman with her deep olive skin, waist-length dark hair, and stripper-fit body, but it took more than good looks to pique my interest.

She hadn't mentioned anything about her attack tonight, too busy concentrating on winning my affections. I liked Leandra as a person, respected her for the lengths she would go through to protect the DeLuca name, but a romance with her was never, nor would it ever be in the cards.

"Can we talk alone? I have a few updates I need to give you."

I nodded, reading her lips since only half her words cut through the noise. She turned and headed towards the area in the back of the club where the offices were located.

We ducked into the second door down the hall, one of the small stockrooms. Once inside, she stood in place, staring me down from head to toe.

"Did you hear about what happened to me tonight?"

"I heard."

I hoped my usual unbothered expression didn't make me come off as an insensitive prick. Although I cared about her well-being as much as any of my men, all I wanted at this point was for her to relay the information and go on about her business after I mapped out a quick plan.

"They were in a dark SUV. It could have been a Jeep. I didn't get a look at any of their faces or anything. You think it has something to do with what happened in Italy to Don Ermanno?"

"I'll have to investigate, but it's possible. I'll have Lenni and Umberto shadow you for a while and make sure this wasn't something random."

"Thank you, Primo. I appreciate that. What about you? The bruise on the side of your head is saying that you may have encountered some trouble tonight yourself?"

"I'm fine. Minor car crash. A few scratches and bruises, nothing detrimental to my health."

When I didn't offer more, she stood there staring before her face lit up with an idea I was sure I didn't want to hear.

"You thought about what I proposed?"

My jaw clenched tight against the amount of effort it took to stop myself from sighing in frustration.

"I don't need or want a girlfriend, woman, or wife. I have too much going on in my life right now. Besides, Emmanuelle treated me like his brother, and I have too much respect for him to be anything other than respectful towards you."

"It's been two years. He would have wanted me to be happy. And I'd just be there if you needed me. A relationship of convenience type of situation."

Her mouth said one thing, but her eyes begged for the opposite. If she hadn't been a woman or a DeLuca, my *fuck you* attitude would have been expressed with more gusto.

However savage we were, we took pride in maintaining a certain level of respect for women. In my case, I did my best to show that sparks of kindness still resided within me even though I wasn't raised right.

I lifted my hand and released three quick snaps in front of Leandra's face to stop her lust induced gaze from roaming my body.

"Leandra. Focus. Is there anything else?"

I knew I looked good. My ego wouldn't accept any other description of myself. However, Leandra was doing way too much for my attention. Even if I were interested in her, the desperation she displayed where it concerned me was a turnoff.

She nodded dejectedly. "I overheard some chatter while I was getting my hair done a few days ago. It sounded like members of the Soldanos family were eager for a power play, specifically for the plot of territory down in Glasgow Village at the Mississippi River since it was once theirs. You want me to befriend one of the men, see if I can get more information?"

"No. I'll look into it. We need to find out who came after you and why before we send you on a covert operation."

"I've done some spy work for Emmanuelle before," she informed with pride.

"And I respect that you would put yourself on the line for this family, but for now, keep your ears open and yourself out of the way of danger."

I believed she got off on the danger, but the last thing I wanted was for her to end up on the wrong side of death on my watch and by my orders.

"Thank you," I cut off whatever she was about to say before turning and walking away.

Chapter Three

Nevah

A night out with my friends, Tracy Monroe and Maya Daniels, was a task much like the one job you needed to do but dreaded the most. Each time I denied their requests to go and shake my ass in front of strange men, they accused me of being stuck up and antisocial.

So what if I was a bit reserved? I grew up in one of the toughest neighborhoods in the city and had managed to claw my way out of it without ending up shot, pregnant, raped, or mentally insane. In my opinion, I deserved to chill and be as boring as I desired.

However, I indulged my friends' requests at least once a month. Wasn't that enough?

I preferred to spend my days off binge-watching television or playing bingo at the nursing home my mother, Vivian Moore, resided in.

Tracy, because she was the married one of the three of us, was using the 'girls' out' time to get away from her husband and three kids. Maya was the opposite of me and Tracy. She picked up and dropped men like she was testing fruit at a supermarket.

Our birthdays were all a month apart, me in April, Tracy in May, and Maya in June. We celebrated our thirtieth in an all-inclusive spa resort in Jamaica last month in June. While drunk off my ass, I made the resolution to be more outgoing. Now, here I was, begrudgingly keeping my word and entertaining their request.

I met Tracy and Maya in college, my freshman year, during our pre-processing weekend twelve years ago, and we've been as tight as the calf muscles on an Olympic sprinter ever since.

"Nevah, meet Ken, Ken, Nevah." Maya introduced her newest victim, shouting over the music before they sat on one of the couches in our cozy corner.

As always, I was nursing a drink before taking one of the two dances I would allot myself as a show of participation. Tracy was out on the dance floor, dropping it like she wasn't married with children, but I knew her well enough to know that all she would do was drink and dance.

Maya's new hookup, who sat between us, leaned closer and whisper-shouted in my ear, "So how about a threesome? You're hot."

Instead of answering him, I sat my unblinking gaze on Maya. If she insisted on picking up these club hounds, the least she could do was make better choices.

I leaned across the man to get closer to Maya's ear and to make sure he heard my comment.

"Put your mangy stray on a leash before I neuter him and lock him in a cage until he learns better manners."

I may have been the quiet friend, but I wasn't anyone's pushover.

The man's eyes bucked at my comment. The statement made him sit his ass up straighter before he cast a questioning glance at Maya. She waved her hand in a sweeping motion away from her body, her gaze locked on his.

"We were going to have some very disrespectful sex, but the one thing you can't do is disrespect my friend. Shoo, fly, you've bothered the wrong person."

She flicked the man away with her hand while keeping her unflinching gaze pinned on his. He had the nerve to look upset at her dismissal.

"How are you just going to reject me?" he asked, eyeballing her. "You aren't even that cute."

She smiled away what he assumed was an insult. If there was one thing I knew about Maya, she didn't lack self-confidence. She invested gym time, salon time, and enough grooming time to her five-seven body to draw attention no matter where she went.

Her honey-hued skin tone and head full of thickly coiled dark hair also drew attention. In her head, she was too good for every man in the building and didn't hesitate to use them as one would a box of Kleenex.

When the man didn't leave after her dismissal, she set her sights on one of the guys who'd walked into the club with him. She called the man closer with a wave of her finger. He came willingly with a huge shit-eating grin plastered on his face. He didn't even cast a glance at his friend who sat next to Maya wearing shock like an expensive suit.

"If I'm not back in fifteen minutes, call the fire department to come and put this one out." She motioned her head to the man reaching down for her hand to help her up. The asshole who asked for the threesome was so outdone, he hopped up and stormed off, muttering something about a "bunch of raggedy bitches."

I stood, prepared to stop Maya from making a drunken decision she would ask for details about tomorrow. Before I could stop her and the man's movement, a group of four stumbled into our corner and bumped me back into my seat, where I landed with a huff of frustration.

The minor setback caused me to lose track of Maya's movements with her new part-time lover. My motherly instincts insisted that she'd drank too much to make sound decisions. Not to mention, she made me nervous with the way she ran through men like she was on some type of mission she hadn't told me and Tracy about.

Once I broke through the crowd of swirling bodies, I raced away from our corner, abandoning it to the drunken group. Maya was nowhere in sight, so I veered in the general direction I assumed they had gone.

A bump, thump, waist squeeze, and a growl all greeted me while I threaded through the hyped-up crowd. I could have doubled as a pinball, but the jostling had no effect on my search efforts.

After a once-over of the wide expanse of the establishment and a scanning stroll down the hall that led to the restrooms, it was beginning to look like my hunt was in vain. This was why I didn't like going out. I spent more time stressed about my friends than I did mingling and connecting.

This wasn't the first time Maya had run off with a man the same night she met him. However, this was the first time she hadn't waited until she left the club. The music in the back office area I loitered in was at the most optimal setting, allowing me a chance to hear myself think.

"Maya," I whispered before opening a door and peeking into an office space marked, "Staff Only." The next three rooms were empty, so I continued my quest to see what was behind the next door.

I prayed I didn't see my friend engaged in a sexual act. Maya was my girl, but I didn't want to see that much of her.

This time, I didn't even bother knocking. I twisted the handle on the door and peeked inside. I inhaled deeply, preparing to call out for Maya. Instead of my friend, I was met with at least ten pairs of intrigued eyes attached to tall, well-built, and very imposing male bodies.

The majority of the men were draped in nice expensive suits, all appeared fit, and the sight of a pistol resting inside one's exposed shoulder holster screamed *danger!*

My heart rate shot through the roof, and for the life of me, my damn brain refused to relay the message to my body. *Back up, close the door, and run.*

The man whose pistol was on display wasn't a detective, although his probing gaze studied me like one.

"Come in," a voice called out before my hand and mind connected and produced the action that would have pulled the door back closed.

"Sorry, I didn't mean to disturb you." I muttered my shaky words, hoping to walk away in peace but sensed that I was disturbing something of great importance.

The tension in the room was thick enough to stifle my next breath. My muscles clenched so tightly, I half expected my body to snap. The sixth sense I relied on growing up said that this was not a *normal* group of men and not an ordinary business meeting. Although there were lights on inside the room, they gave off a dim glow as if setting the mood for their discussion.

The big man flashing the pistol stepped away from the group. With his menacing gaze set on me, he rushed in my direction. Stuck, my grip tightened around the door handle. Lips parted, my heartbeat pounded loud in my ears and my quick breaths only managed to make it half way down my throat before rushing back out.

A big hand gripped my arm so firmly, it caused me to wince before I was dragged into the room with my heels scraping the floor. When the door slammed behind me, the hard sound added fuel to my flaming fears and caused prayers to instantly consume my thoughts.

According to the group's intimidating demeanor and sharp-eyed glares, I was standing in a den of vipers.

"Take your hands off of her," a strong male voice called out, the sound piercing the air like a violent lightning strike. The strong hand gripping my arm let go, and lifted in surrender. Every other big body inside the room grew as tense as I was rigid.

"Do you know this woman?" another of the men asked, glancing at the tall man cast in shadow due to the light shining at his back. Though I believed he had spoken in my defense, the level of dark terror he gave off made the walls in the large room close in on me.

Why did everyone, including me, hold our breaths while awaiting his answer?

Except for the one standing next to me, the men stood in a wide circle, their gazes bouncing back and forth between me and the man who spoke those forceful words in my defense.

The dark, energetic shadow didn't answer but reached out a hand. Even from across the room, I didn't miss that his shadowed hand was unmistakably aimed in my direction, palm up. The sight of him reaching out to *me* sent terror shrieking through me so forcefully, I trembled.

Based on the humbling behavior of the men surrounding him, he was their leader. I didn't know this man from Adam but had enough good sense to know I needed to take his hand. I sensed he didn't offer up goodwill gestures often, if ever. My problem? I didn't know if I was being rescued or dragged deeper into pure, unfiltered darkness.

I reached out for his hand, and although a light tremble shot through my legs, something about his prolonged gesture suggested I could trust him. It was buried deep in his admiring gaze.

When I stepped close enough to see the other elements reflected in those eyes, genuine sincerity surrounded by danger and intrigue was reflected back to me.

He closed his big, warm hand around mine, and the next thing I knew, I was being drawn into his solid body so rapidly, I lost my breath from the firm impact. A rush of panic, excitement, and intrigue snatched the last remnants of mental strength I had left.

Now, I was cast out in a vast uncharted sea with no mental or physical blankets of strength to protect me. The first knowing signs of reality that hit me wasn't at all what I expected. The scent coming off this man called to my deeply buried erotic impulses regardless of the situation.

The smell was dark and spicy with a hint of ginger and piney woods and so potent, I inhaled deeply. I managed to get a grip on my senses and snapped my eyes open.

What the hell is wrong with me?

Since my face was positioned so close to his, my eyes a few inches below his, the view reeled me in, putting a death-grip on the little bit of focus I reclaimed.

My first up-close look at this man had me swallowing a big gulp of *holy shit!* He was as sinfully intriguing as his scent. I felt caught, trapped in muted helplessness. Why wasn't I scared or was I?

The sharp breath I gulped down gave me enough strength to lift my eyes again, but I refused to by-pass the sexy lines of his lips. My curious gaze traced along the curves of those lips that formed their own language of seduction without a single syllable passing through them.

My gaze swept over his thick, dark beard and kept going down and back up until I found deep-set penetrating gray eyes with the ability to hold me captive. His eyes remained locked on mine, and call me crazy, but there was a sense of knowing lingering in them.

Who was this? Why was he holding me like we were acquainted? Why was he staring me down with that big smile in his eyes that didn't touch his lips?

I had no choice but to succumb to the strong power of his impacting caress and to the tight muscles of his arm pressed against my back. His caressing warmth made me melt, but there was more to our connection when I grasped that my arms were wrapped around his torso as tightly as his were wrapped around me.

His body was a mass of lean muscle, just waiting to be admired. Movement in my peripheral vision called my attention away from what I knew was a chiseled jawline under his thick beard.

The men hadn't said a word in protest of our actions, although I sensed my presence made the situation inside this room intensify tenfold. Not even the deliberate clearing of a throat had disturbed our introductory caress.

Why hadn't I let go of him yet? My inner voice yelled, "*Back away now!*" and the rest of me said, "*No way in hell am I letting go of this.*"

My *hero* didn't ease the hold he had on me, nor did he remove his gaze from mine until my arms slackened around his waist. It was the only resisting front I could muster.

When he finally decided to release me from the intoxicating tightness of his grip, he didn't let me go too far. He took his time, turning me slightly with a firm hand so that I was aligned with his side.

Arm wrapped securely around my waist, he kept me pinned against his side so that I faced the men. Was he nonverbally introducing me to them?

Oddly, I felt safe. Protected, even. We didn't even know each other's names, but it didn't stop whatever this connection was between us. He hadn't uttered a word to me yet, but I acknowledged that I was intimately immersed in his world.

When I managed to pull my gaze away from him a second time, the group stared at us like a miracle was being performed. Eyes unblinking, lips parted, and eyebrows lifted high. A few gave each other questioning glances, hoping for an explanation.

The fear my dark savior had managed to coax away rushed back at the sight of all those eyes aimed in our direction. The lump of, *oh shit*, I thought I swallowed a moment ago was still stuck in my throat.

"Are we going to continue?" one of the men asked with his gaze pinned on me. The hard stares the group raked me up and down with produced a dangerous vibe that made me squirm. I was the minority in this room based on gender and race, and although I was profiled in shopping centers and while driving, I couldn't recall experiencing this level of intimidation.

The men were hesitant about speaking with me in this room. A few started to speak but managed only nonverbal utterances before giving up. I believed they feared who I *still* had my arms wrapped around more than they did my presence.

The way their eyes begged him for answers confirmed my thoughts. A quick glance up at my dark champion showed him scanning the circle of men, his chin hiked up with an air of authority.

"If she were a threat, she sure as hell wouldn't be standing here," he responded to the stares, patting one of his big hands against my waist and inadvertently making my insides quiver.

His words alone eased the heavy coat of tension in the room. Shoulders visibly dropped and the suffocating tightness closing in on me eased to a tolerable level.

"You're our Capo. We can't let you go off alone now that we know you've been tagged by The Malizioso," one man stated. He was being careful with his words based on the way his gaze kept bouncing between me and the man literally wearing me as his newest accessory.

"And I won't have someone up my ass twenty-four-seven. I can't and won't operate that way. The Malizioso has a set of rules just like us. If you kill the one who they've deployed to take you out, the hit is null and void."

Wait. What?

My head jerked at the notion of what my brain was processing. Did I just hear that my new sexy savior has a hit out on him? My eyes crept up to his face where his penetrating gaze waited to meet mine. I was searching for answers in his eyes since a verbal connection hadn't been established between us.

If the man helping me was wanted, then what did that say about the rest of them? *Jesus.* What had I stepped into when I opened that door?

"In your case, it may mean several hitmen," the man with his hair graying at the temples replied. His words made the question circling my brain resurface.

Who the hell was I all boo'd up with? What kind of meeting had I accidentally interrupted? If someone was gunning for this man, I didn't want to be near him when they found him. The idea that he wasn't the least bit bothered that there was a bounty on his head made me further question his identity.

Upon further inspection, I didn't miss the sight of more guns flashing like twinkling stars with each man's movement. Due to my presence, some began communicating in Italian, leaving me to pick out the few words I understood until *Don* Ermanno was mentioned.

Was this the *mob*? Had I walked in on a mob meeting in progress? If my speculations were true, I'd stepped in shit so deep, I might as well train myself to get used to the scent.

Chapter Four

Primo

The meeting was being carried out with a cryptic vibe despite my implied warning on the contrary to the men about my new woman. However, in this case, it was a good thing they hadn't listened.

Was I insanely attracted to this woman who literally walked in and called out to me in a language I didn't understand but had enough sense to hear? Fucking right I was. I had to be if I were willing to continue with the meeting as though nothing had changed. I didn't know a damn thing about her, yet I couldn't help keeping an arm wrapped securely around her waist.

She could have been the hitter The Malizioso sent to kill me. However, my ability to read people hadn't failed me yet, and it said she wasn't a threat. Her hold on me had loosened but she hadn't let go, a revealing action that implied that our instant attraction was mutual.

Allowing her to stay for the rest of our meeting was an action that outweighed my words. The men in this room rarely saw me with a woman, much less claiming one as emphatically as I was this one.

Their minds were blown to hell and back, and by continuing my uncharacteristic actions, they remained on edge. I read the questions in their inquisitive gazes, but they trusted the strength of my leadership enough to proceed, despite their predatory instincts.

Other than who hired a hitman to kill me, there was another question on my mind I needed to answer. *What was it about this particular woman that had me breaking my own rules?* Though it wasn't a written one, I would have chewed off the head of any of my men for pulling a stunt like this.

My gaze dropped away from the person speaking, and big, innocent brown eyes met mine with interest and questions blazing in their compelling depths. She understood that she had walked into the wrong room based on the sorrow reflecting in her gaze and the stress etched in the subtle creases of her face and stiff body. I sensed her intense train of thought and tasted hints of her fear on my tongue, but she managed to keep it in check enough to show me that her strengths outweighed her fears.

"I believe you need to consider the protection detail, Capo," Fernando insisted with his palms up. I shook my head at the suggestion.

"Like I mentioned earlier, all I need to do is kill the one or more coming for me—before they kill me."

My arrogance was showing, but I didn't know any other way. However, by claiming the sexy woman in my arms, I was inadvertently drawing her into my world, creating an even bigger mess. At this moment, I wasn't altogether sure if I was helping her or sentencing her to a life of unadulterated savagery. All I knew was that I didn't want anyone else's hands on her for any reason.

Helpless to stop it, my gaze dropped and lingered on her before I gave a little squeeze to her waist to ease her tension. She was one of the most gorgeous women I ever encountered and that was saying a lot considering women came a dime a dozen in our world.

I sensed the invisible rays of light shining within her, the glow of their warmth breezing along my skin. The goodness she possessed was pulling my darkness in like a high-powered vacuum set on maximum suction. Hidden deep under her glow, I spotted the glimmers of darkness she possessed. She hadn't lived a sheltered life.

Despite all the drama, the hit out on me, and the death of my late Don, a rare urge to smile took over whenever she filled my view. Her skin, like warm, flowing maple syrup, cast a refreshing glow against the lighting in the room. She projected an angelic radiance that kept stealing my attention as much as those big brown eyes of hers.

Her hair was up in a neat bun pinned at the crown of her head, disguising its true length. The style added an elegance to her appearance that I rarely saw in a club setting. Her overall style was flirty-sexy, giving just enough to show that she was a sexy woman, while tempting your desire to see more. She wore faded, ripped jeans, sassy black heels, and a stylish multi-colored top that highlighted her tall, sexy frame.

In heels, she was about three inches shorter than my six-foot-three height, an indication that she was at least five-eight. She gave off that fresh-from-the-shower scent, an invigorating mix of honey blossoms kissed by the remnants of a good dream.

Her appearance kept me intrigued, and although the men were tense about her presence, I hadn't missed the admiring glimpses that strayed in her direction and lingered when they thought I wasn't paying attention.

This strange pull she had on me was something I had never encountered. Therefore, I couldn't apply reasoning for it to make sense. I hadn't determined yet if it was a problem.

For her sake and mine, I couldn't afford to be distracted, yet I did nothing to talk myself out of this situation. I didn't even know this woman's name, and she was managing to do what no other ever had—draw my undivided attention.

She could have stumbled into many places but had somehow landed in a room filled with savage killers. In a way, I felt sorry for her, an emotion I'd learned to suppress.

Without any convincing on her part, I placed her on a pedestal that told my guys she was important enough for them to respect. My stance with her, whether she realized it or not, made her one of the most targeted, protected, and spotlighted women in St. Louis.

She had no idea she was in the arms of "Hades," the name people sometimes used when they referred to me. The name represented how often I served up death, delivering unexpected and mostly horrific endings to those unlucky enough to land in my path.

"I've heard enough," I stated, breaking into a complaint Orlando had managed to wrap in a neatly veiled suggestion. There were times the men would complain about the most menial things, aware they would get ignored. It was also their way of checking to see if I would consider their point valid enough for more attention.

Since I only gave them one chance to mess up, they were careful in how they conducted business. One costly slip resulting in someone's health or life, and I sentenced them to my death chambers.

The chambers were two soundless, dark, and cold underground rooms the men would earn time inside. Of all the punishments I endured during my training, and once when I was captured, the dark emptiness of being trapped with my own mind was the worst. The mind-torture far exceeded any physical pain I ever suffered.

My chambers worked wonders on the men who visited them as they did everything in their power to avoid returning. Not to mention the parting gift I gave them when their stint was done. I gave them the choice to pick a finger, ear, tongue, nipple, or toe, the part didn't matter, but they would lose something as a reminder to never fuck up again.

The tips of my ring and pinky fingers on my right hand had been hacked off with a rusty bone saw. Therefore, I knew the value of loss and would never do to my men what I hadn't already endured. Experience on both sides of punishment taught me that it was one of the best motivational tools.

The ten men who had been *motivated* during my reign as Capo, so far, were now among the best at their jobs and often given more authority because they were most likely to succeed. They were also the best advocates for assuring that others did their jobs well.

Years before I was Capo, and up until his death, I, along with three others, worked exclusively for our late Don Ermanno. For the past two years, there were times I pulled double duty when an order came directly from the Don.

The work was what I liked to call mafia black-ops, which included off-the-book operations that benefited the family. The details of my assignments were never disclosed to the family, and in most cases, they didn't know anything had ever occurred.

The men didn't question me when I gave weak excuses and disappeared for days and sometimes weeks at a time. They naturally assumed I was handling Capo business, the job a suitable cover for what I had *really* been trained to become—a DeLuca assassin.

The news of my hit resurfaced and blasted away my raging thoughts. There was also the new lady in my life who I too easily volunteered to take responsibility for. The timing was fucked up, but I wanted her and somehow sensed that the attraction was more than sexual. Some force within me had zeroed in on her like a heat-seeking missile. Now that the connection had been acknowledged, I didn't know how to disconnect.

All I needed to do now was figure out how to work all this shit out without fucking up the world and killing everyone who spiked my suspicions from Missouri all the way to Sicily.

Chapter Five

Nevah

What...the...hell?

I knew of the mob through whispers and my friends pointing out members when we encountered them in public, but I had never been this up close and personal. The rumors alone were enough to make a grown man run and hide.

Now, here I was, pressed into the side of one who, based on the way the other men regarded him, was as dangerous as the Black Plague. He dismissed the men after several repeated attempts to warn him about taking precautions against the hit out on him.

Once the last man filed out and pulled the door closed behind him, a set of intrigued eyes fell on me. Like the fool I had apparently become in his presence, I allowed myself to get lost in his striking eyes that appeared gray at first glance. However, they were a beautiful mix of blue, light green, and a variation of grays that looked like a storm of colors was raging in his eyes.

The logical part of my brain kept warning me that he was the walking manifestation of danger, but I couldn't help admiring this up-close view of him. He was…intoxicating, potent in a way that he drew me in with no real effort.

"What's your name?" he asked. He still hadn't released me from his hold.

His accent was pronounced, letting me know he wasn't originally from the states.

"Nevah," I stated, surprising myself by how calm I sounded despite my heart attempting to stomp a hole through my chest.

"Nevah, I'm Primo DeLuca, and whatever you've heard about the DeLuca family is probably true. When you opened that door and peeked into this room, you changed your whole life within seconds."

"What? What do you mean, I changed my life? It was an honest mistake. I was searching for my friend."

"As unintentional as the action was, it doesn't matter. If I hadn't claimed you as my woman when I did, do you have any idea what could have happened to you for walking in on a meeting like ours?"

I swallowed; sure he could read the thoughts shining through my wide, unblinking gaze. *Raped, beaten, strangled, and thrown in the Mississippi River with the fish after a double tap to the back of my head.*

He shook his head like he knew what I was thinking.

"We *are* savages and proud to wear the moniker, but we don't hurt women like you may think. In your case, one of the guys would have found you a job within the organization. Or, one would have claimed you, and you would likely be married as soon as tomorrow."

Speechless. I blinked, the only remaining indication that I wasn't dreaming. He couldn't have been serious.

"Based on what I've learned of our late Don's assassination, there's a killer among us. Since I haven't found out yet who the family traitor is, I couldn't let you end up in the hands of a monster worse than me, now could I?"

The way he worded the question. The way he so easily labeled himself a monster. I was sure I was already in the hands of the devil—a handsome one, but definitely a devil. And despite what he was saying, I didn't believe for a minute any of the others were worse than him.

I pulled from a reserve pocket of strength hidden deep within my bones, enough to at least speak.

"I appreciate you stepping in and helping me, but what happens now? I have a life, work, friends who are probably out there searching for me. My mother's in a nursing home. She's my dependent. I can't just say 'bye-bye' to my life. I have responsibilities."

"For now, you're stuck with me until I figure out a way to get you back to your life."

"I can't be stuck with you. They said you had a hit out on you, and you said it yourself that there's strife within your family. You don't trust anyone right now, especially family members. Wouldn't I be safer on my own?"

"We have a lot of enemies out there, and with a traitorous killer loose within my own family, our relationship could already be spread halfway around the planet. If that's the case, you're already as big a target as me, if not bigger."

He said, *our relationship,* like we were a real couple. And how on earth had I become a target in fifteen-minutes?

"There's no guarantee that anyone knows about me. No one has seen me with you except the men inside this room. You're obviously their boss, so why can't you just let me go and pretend like this never happened?"

"It goes much deeper than you think. One of the men standing in this room tonight may be the traitor. The moment the men saw the way I was holding on to you, you automatically became one of two things: a target for attack to hurt or get to me, or you fell under their protection."

He held up a finger to drive home another point. "The loyal ones *will* protect you because of me, and it's not something we take lightly in this family. No matter where you go now, eyes will be on you, and if our eyes are on you, the eyes of our enemy, whether it's a DeLuca or not, will be on you also. This situation is not something I can take back, and neither can you."

My breathing sped up and this time it wasn't because of this man's attractiveness. Panic tightened the already tense set of my face and deepened my frown.

"Please. If you're in charge, can't you do something? I can't give up my life because I mistakenly opened a door that *should* have been locked. It's not fair, and the more we talk about this, the more I'm starting to think you're feeding me a bunch of crap. For all I know, you could be one of those guys that traps women and turns them into your bottom bitch."

Irritation about this whole crazy-ass situation was plucking my nerves. I only cursed when I was upset and listening to this man tell me I didn't have a way out of this situation was ticking me off.

His right brow shot up at my rant, but he continued to stare down on me without replying. Memories from my past surfaced, reminding me that I wasn't easily bullied. I had grown up in one of the most dangerous, gutter-ass neighborhoods in the city with a crack addict mother most of my life. Now this man had the audacity to tell me I needed to rearrange my life over an innocent mistake.

Nope.

"I'm going to find my friends and go home. You can tell your men we broke up or something. Or better yet, why don't you call me once you're off that hit list."

We both knew he didn't have my phone number, and the hit list jab was a bit insensitive but a fitting reminder of the danger awaiting.

His eyes gave away nothing, but the little twitch my comments put on his lips had me fighting to restrain my own stupid smile. Under a different set of circumstances, I would have tossed all my inhibitions in the trash can for this man.

Finally, I found the strength to break the hold he had on me and backed away. I turned quickly, my heels giving the floor a little departing scrape before I strolled towards the door, praying he wouldn't stop me. A quick glance back showed him standing in place, with an unbothered expression on his handsome face.

Once I was outside the door, I walked briskly back to the sound of the pounding drum beats pouring over dancing bodies. The reason I had ventured to the back of this club in the first place resurfaced. Where the hell had Maya gone with that guy?

After a few frantic minutes of searching the sitting areas and restrooms again, I found Tracy chatting it up with a hot Hispanic guy with a neat goatee surrounding a set of sexy, pouty lips.

Tracy's eyes widened when she noticed me approaching. She hopped up, not caring that the man was in the middle of a sentence. Her eyes were alight with relief.

"Girl, where the hell have you been?"

"I went after Maya to stop her from doing something she might regret later."

She waved my comment away, her gaze flicking in the direction of the bar.

"You wasted your time. Maya is being Maya. She got rid of date number two and is at the bar working on number four by now."

My eyes slid closed on a long-winded sigh. All that had occurred in the past twenty minutes flooded my brain. I squeezed my eyes tight, the lids fluttering with stress while I shook my head to chase away the memories.

I opened my eyes to Tracy giving me the "spill it" eyes, reading whatever my expression was projecting. The guy she was stringing along stood and tapped her shoulder, attempting to reclaim her attention. She shrugged his hand away when he tried to touch her again. Luckily, he took the hint and sat back down.

"I've had one hell of an interesting night. I'll tell you about it tomorrow. I'm about to order an Uber and head home."

Her head shook, and the deep furrow between her eyes highlighted her disapproval of my decision.

"It's not even eleven yet. You haven't even let any of these guys see the great ass you've got. Did you even *try* to trap them with those big puppy dog eyes of yours and get at least a few free drinks?"

She glanced back at the smiling face of her date, whose eyes were aimed at her ass in her black, form-fitting dress that flowed along her body like it was painted on. Little did her temporary date know, he wasn't going to even get a whiff of what he was drooling over.

My head was moving in the negative before she started her attempts to convince me to stay.

"I'm going," I insisted, then softened my voice. "Will you text me later to let me know you two made it home safely?"

Tracy pursed her lips and nodded, knowing that once my mind was made up, there was no changing it. She reached for my hand, giving it a caring squeeze. Her brows lifted high, showing me two sad begging eyes, but the expression wasn't powerful enough to make me stay.

I turned and stepped away with the weight of tonight's events on my shoulders. Was it even necessary for me to tell my friends about what I had stepped into tonight? What purpose would it serve other than to give them something else to worry about?

Tracy and Maya assumed I was lonely since I rarely did anything outside of work and hung out with them from time to time. I had overheard them saying as much but hadn't taken offense since it was partially true. Their answer to fix what they assumed was my problem was to stick a man into my situation.

I did get lonely for male company. However, the prospect of forging a relationship had always been a daunting task. Did I want one? *Yes.* Did I want to go through the process of getting to know someone? *Hell No.*

Men, the ones I often encountered, were tools. I had run the gauntlet of them—the cheaters and the misogynistic pigs. The ones who pretended to be the best thing since sliced bread when they were actually burnt toast.

The worst monster I was involved with was the one I had foolishly married behind my friend's back. A month into our union I was forced to find a way to get rid of him. It had taken time to uncover his abusive nature and that he had served five years on an attempted murder charge.

My naivety had led me to believe that an older man could help solve all my problems.

Amid the drama of my younger years, I had also taken on the financial responsibility of providing care for my mother, not that she deserved my dedication based on the way she treated me growing up.

Neglect, hunger, and beatings were the ways she had shown me attention. She teased me incessantly about naming me Nevah Moore, saying after she had me, she was *never* having any *more* babies. The joke was on her because most people liked the name.

After my thirteenth birthday, the abuse she dished out intensified. Her slaps and name-calling turned into kicks and punches. Due to years of drug abuse, my mother ended up suffering a massive stroke at forty that left her unable to walk or talk.

She became my dependent and I was forced to work two jobs from the time I was seventeen, throughout college, and a few years beyond, just to afford a decent nursing home for her.

The energetic bodies bumping into me pulled me back to my current reality. I tossed a final glance across my shoulder at Tracy before I was folded into the crowd. The multiple points of constant contact caused me to jerk towards my destination like I was in the midst of doing an awkward dance move.

I appreciated my friends campaigning for my social life but going out with them usually ended with me attempting to save them from situations they would have been involved in regardless.

Halfway to my destination, the friend in me wouldn't let me leave without looking back in Maya's direction. After craning my neck for what felt like an hour, I spotted her near the bar like Tracy had informed.

Guilt slammed into me and my quick steps stalled, causing people to bump into me harder, some belting out their frustration. I turned in the opposite direction, praying I didn't regret this last minute decision. I was about to risk being caught by a mafia boss to check on my friend.

Dammit!

Maya acted tough but had a heart of gold that she only allowed me and Tracy to see. She was more determined than the rest of us not to show weakness. However, I knew her pain.

She was still suffering the loss of her brother whose death seven months ago had wreaked her. What made the situation worse, the police weren't doing anything that we could tell, to solve his murder.

The closer I stepped to Maya and her newest victim for the night, the more my eyes squinted. The man looked familiar and she and he appeared to be in the midst of an argument.

Shit!

"Look B3co or whatever your name is…" I caught the first part of her condescending sentence, despite the crowd-noise. "I don't care if this club belongs to the Pope, I'll ask whoever I want, whatever I want," Maya spit more of her vicious words at the man.

She stared him down like he was the short one, despite him towering over her with a strained grimace on his face.

"I'll pick you up and carry you out of here myself if you're here to start trouble," he spat back at her.

The dark haired man took a threatening step closer to her, but thankfully didn't attempt to make good on his comment. I pushed my way through the last of the crowd that seemed to be holding me back despite my determined pace.

Now that I clearly saw his face, the man looked familiar to me because I had just seen him less than twenty-five minutes ago. He was one of the men who were in that mob meeting I had accidentally stepped into, while searching for Maya. I needed to get her away from him before we ended up with more mob energy than we could handle aimed at us.

"Is everything okay?" I questioned, walking up to Maya and standing beside her. My shoulder edged out in front of hers like a mother readying herself to protect her baby although I'm sure Maya was a lot more scrappy than me.

The man standing before us was just as imposing as Primo DeLuca. I seriously doubted that me and Maya had a chance against him if he decided he wanted to do bad things to us. When he managed to pull his gaze away from Maya's threatening one, recognition flashed in his eyes at the sight of me.

"Everything is fine. I'm just playing the part of the Peacekeeper, so your friend here will stop stirring up trouble in my club. She's agitating my customers." His eyes were back on Maya before he completed the statement.

"I'm sorry to hear that," I offered him, before snatching Maya by the arm and dragging her off towards the restroom area. As soon as we hit the dimly lit hall and the tone of the music lowered, I swung her around to face me like a mother about to discipline her child.

"Maya, what the hell? Do you have any idea who you were arguing with?"

She shrugged.

"He thinks just because he owns this club, he could tell me who to talk to. Acting like he's my keeper or something."

My head shook with slow disapproval. The only reason I wasn't yelling at Maya right now was because I understood her pain.

"Please tell me you're not going off on another of your hunting expeditions. It's dangerous and certainly reckless, especially questioning people like you're the police."

"What else am I supposed to do?" She questioned, turning her hands up in surrender. "If I don't do something about my brother's case, it's just going to get tossed like so many others into the cold case files. If it's not already there."

My head dropped a notch and my eyes fell closed.

"I know. Just promise me you'll chill for now. I'll help you like I did before if you don't hear something from the detectives soon. Okay?"

She nodded. The sadness she tried but failed to keep out of her eyes burst free. After a moment of deaf silence passed between us, she threw her arms around my neck.

"Thank you," she whisper-talked, her words coming out harsh and louder than I'm sure she intended. Her fruit and alcohol smelling breath blew in my face.

"You and Tracy are the only ones who care," her voice cracked.

After their parent's death, Maya, at two months shy of eighteen, was left to raise her eleven year old brother. He had been like a son to her and was all she had left as far as blood.

She had more family in the city, a few aunts, an uncle, and some cousins but she had disowned them. Most of them proudly lived off of public assistance and none bothered to lift a finger to help Maya when she was struggling to raise her brother.

"I'm going to get an Uber and go home," I said, dispelling my runaway thoughts. "Try to have fun tonight, and please text me when you and Tracy make it home."

She didn't even try to talk me out of leaving early. With her teeth sinking into her bottom lip, she gave a sad nod before I stepped away.

It was time to get out of this place and put this night behind me. Besides, there was a mob boss in the building who thought I was his woman.

I needed to make my getaway before he found me and tried to lay claim again. The way I saw it, if I left now, Mr. Sexy DeLuca would have no idea where I went, and as depressing as the notion was, I would never see him again.

I ordered my Uber while walking towards the front door. A smile slid across my lips when the app showed me that one was ten minutes away from the location I requested to be picked up. The corner of Chestnut and Bittle was a few blocks away and parallel to this club, which left me more than enough time to make it to my location.

I pushed past the crowd near the door and stepped into the long hallway that led to the exit. The dim setting gave the space an eerie vibe and had me speed-walking to make it to the exit. Heavy footsteps approaching from behind put an anxious tingle in my spine and caused my shoulders to tense.

Unable to help myself, a glance back showed a tall guy in a suit whose face was shaded by shadows. His solid build reminded me of Primo, but there was no mistaking *him*. Primo had that vibe that let you know you were flirting with danger. He possessed the kind of dark passion that drew you in like a strong drug because he was so damned sexy and confident.

My footsteps quickened, the beat pumping as fast as my heart hammered. Did the man's steps pick up also or was I just paranoid?

I maintained my rapid pace and was reaching out for the front door's push-bar seconds before I got there. The door sprang open from the hard push I delivered. The twinkling night outside, along with the crush of dancing bodies on the sidewalk filled my view. Relief brushed away the panic racing through me.

Despite the fading sound of his footsteps, the tall man continued to approach behind me. Could Primo have been right about me having eyes on me already?

I sped past the threshold of the door that spit me out onto the sidewalk's high traffic zone. A satisfied smirk surfaced once I was safely outside, and the *thump* of quick-moving bodies met mine.

If the big guy from the hall was following me, he was shit-out-of-luck now because I was quickly sucked into the crowd. A deep sigh of relief rushed out before I glanced down to check the status of my Uber.

"Thank you, Lord," I breathed out. For a minute, I was afraid I would end up tied to a mob boss.

I approached the crosswalk that led to my stop with twenty seconds left on the countdown time remaining to cross the street. Me and about eight others marched across the intersection, my heels attacking the pavement with each of my quick steps.

Instead of standing near the busy intersection, I eased back into the shadows of the nearest building. The edgy prickling along my spine while leaving the club hadn't dissipated and had me glancing around like a paranoid addict.

The streetlights and headlights blended and illuminated the surrounding area. A distant view showed only dark blurs of movement, like the light clung to only the most active areas.

My fidgety fingers and feet stopped tapping when the shape of the gray Camry I was expecting came into view. It made its approach through the energetic flow of traffic.

A smile stretched wide across my face, my mind already on the bag of salty-sweet popcorn and the newest show I planned on binging. When the Camry pulled to a stop at the edge of the sidewalk behind a big black SUV, I stepped away from the shadows.

I reached for the back passenger door handle with a relieving smile filling my face. My rejoicing moments came to an abrupt stop when a strong hand locked around my wrist, out of nowhere. A long-winded gasp inflated my lungs, my body heaving, and my eyes wide. I stumbled over my words before spitting out a few.

"What? Who? Let me go!" I yelled, attempting to yank my arm from the man's vise grip.

"I'm your protection," was what I thought he said.

Damn what he said. A killer would say anything to gain your trust. With me locked in his tight grip, he knocked on the front window of my Uber, so hard I expected the glass to break.

The window came down, and the driver bent and peered up at the big bulky white guy effortlessly holding me in place while I struggled to break free. My fingers ached from pulling and clawing to pry his hand from around my arm, but my attempts were useless.

He tossed some bills at the driver. "That's for your trouble. The lady already has a ride," he all but growled at the man.

"No. I don't already have a ride. He's kidnapping me! Call the police!" I shouted, getting the attention of the driver and other passersby.

My shouting made the walkers speed up and zip past us, glancing back with raised brows to avoid my troubles. Their total disregard for my safety caused my rapidly pulsing heart to sink deep into the pit of my stomach. When had the world become so heartless?

The big bully leaned down and peeked into the window at the Uber driver, who looked like he was swallowing rocks at the sight of the bigger man. I wasn't sure what was exchanged between the two, but when my abductor straightened his intimidating posture, the driver screeched away, almost getting hit by an oncoming car.

I continued my useless struggling while being dragged closer to the back of the big black SUV that I should have been more suspicious of when it drove up and parked. The big hulking man with me in his tight grip opened the back door.

It took little effort on his part to manhandle me. First, he spun me to face him before he got a good grip under my arms and lifted me into the back of the vehicle, even as I kicked and screamed like a madwoman.

As soon as my butt landed on the smooth dark leather, my imposing captor climbed in after me. He used his body to shove me further into the vehicle and closed the door.

He didn't say a word but flashed me that glare a mother flashes at a child who's been acting up. The driver was a small figure shrouded in black who merged into traffic with ease.

Why hadn't I listened to Primo? Now, I was being taken and had no idea if it was by his guys or his enemies.

"What do you guys want? I don't know anything. I'm a nurse who works long hours and double shifts because I live a boring life and would rather be at the hospital helping my patients than socializing."

The man lifted a brow while the driver glanced back and winked, revealing that she was a woman.

"We are DeLucas. You're safe with us as long as you're with Primo. But there is no telling what will happen to you if you wander off and end up in the wrong hands."

The news calmed me a little, but a big problem remained. If these guys were who they said they were, it meant Primo had spoken the truth. It meant my whole lifestyle was about to go from boring as hell to hell on earth.

What the hell was I going to do now?

I breathed through my anxiety and did what I did best when I was in a troubling situation. I chanted every motivational saying I knew with prayers thrown into the mix. The mental self-therapy session left me unnervingly still, so much so I sensed my escorts watching me. They probably thought I was crazy.

***

Assassins?

I was usually underestimated because I looked about as innocent as I acted. It was an assumption I preferred. Most people automatically assumed I didn't know certain lingo or street terminology. People who looked at me didn't see someone who knew how to use a gun or could hold my own in a fight.

In the case of my current abductors, I had gathered enough from the big guy's conversation on the phone to know that these two were sister and brother and assassins for the DeLuca family.

The man never outright said the word assassin, but the context clues painted me a clear enough picture. Words and phrases like, receiving assignments, security, lists, and eliminating targets was more than enough for me to jump to my current conclusion. Add to that, he referred to the driver as *"Sis"* in an endearing tone.

In families like this one, the security team was code for killers. And not the lame ass wanna-be killers either. They were the big bad ass ones who wiped out whole families and went out and had drinks afterwards. They were the ones who took out the trash, struck down the family enemies, and provided protection when and wherever the family needed it.

And here I was, plucked from the streets against my will and shoved into the back of what I was willing to bet was a bulletproofed SUV with no idea where I was being taken.

If my heart fisted any harder it would cease up in my chest. I prayed that Primo and I had made a genuine connection and these two were truly members of the DeLuca family, ones who Primo trusted. Otherwise, I was going to have to out think two trained killers to live to see the next day.

"He's an asset until he isn't anymore. We'll need him to provide the codes, after which, he will no longer be of any use to us," the big guy told his sister.

They were talking about whoever he had just been having a phone conversation with.

"I know, but I could use him in the future. You think he'll be more trouble than he's worth if we keep him around longer than we projected?"

Why were they speaking so freely in front of me, not only about who they were in relation to the DeLuca family but who they were planning to take out? Was it because they were planning to kill me and it didn't matter what I knew about them?

The big guy, though sitting in the back with me, was on and off the phone and working on some type of tablet during our drive. Other than communicating on the phone and with his sister, he only cast me a few fleeting glances.

The SUV idled, slowing in this upscale residential neighborhood we were rolling through. My eyes bucked and my head jerked around in every direction, attempting to push my vision through the darkness outside to see landmarks and street signs.

Although I was born and raised in St Louis, I wasn't familiar with this area or neighborhood. I couldn't recall an exit number from the interstate either.

My phone.

They hadn't taken my phone which was still shoved into my back pocket. I could at least be tracked and if given a chance, I could call 911. But was I truly in trouble?

Of course I was in trouble. After walking in on a mob meeting in progress, I was claimed by a mob boss, and was now a hostage to who I assumed were two of the family assassins.

Lord, if you get me out of this one, I promise I'll read the bible more. I'll go to church more. I'll get on my knees and pray more.

The SUV was whipped into the driveway of a large single story brick house and driven around to the garage that was conveniently located at the back of the house.

My breathing started to rush. I chewed hard into my bottom lip, making it slide harshly against the sharp edges of my teeth. Sitting still was out of the question. My neck and body was on a constant swivel, sometimes going in two different directions, my movement was so erratic. The seat squeaked under me while we waited for the garage to lift.

"Stay calm. We are not going to hurt you Nevah," the big guy said before the SUV entered the garage and came to a stop. The garage door began to fall behind us. It was an extra barrier blocking my freedom as far as I was concerned.

The only thing that drew my attention was the man throwing the door open and climbing out. He reached back inside the vehicle to help me out. My gaze dropped to his hand, staring at it like it was a snapping alligator.

He stood patiently waiting until I found the courage to take his hand. I slid to the edge of the seat and allowed my hand to tighten around his before I jumped out of the vehicle.

The sister stood at the door that led into the house with her back to us. She pulled her gun, aiming it skyward before she pushed the door and let it creak open into the shadows inside the house. She glanced back and gave her brother a perceptive nod before she disappeared into the house.

He turned his back to me, facing the exit although the garage door was closed. They were being extra careful and making sure this place was secure.

Gun.

His gun was sitting right there in my face. It was shoved down the back of his pants and so close, all I had to do was lift my hand to touch it.

"All clear!" The sister called, making me jump and snap my eyes away from the big shiny pistol.

We turned in the direction of the entrance and the peculiar behavior of these two just kept getting weirder. It appeared as if the big man was about to be a gentleman and place a hand on my lower back to escort me, but he stopped himself. Instead, he ushered his hand towards the door where his sister waited. The smile in her eyes was small, barely noticeable, but reassuring.

My face squinted, still confused about their purpose with me. They were acting protective over me instead of like people who intended to do me harm.

I forced my legs to move me in the sister's direction, my steps awkward and slow. A little twitch of a smile flashed across the woman's pouty lips.

"Have you decided yet if we're the good guys or the bad guys?" She asked.

"No," I answered, making my approach to the three steps that led into the doorway she stood in.

"You're definitely the bad guys, but if you let me go right now, I'll upgrade your status to *good*-bad guys."

She broke out laughing while stepping aside so that I could walk inside.

"I like you," she said, amusement in her tone. She took the lead getting in front of me.

"Have a seat there. I'll grab you some water. Are you hungry?" she asked while I stepped into the large living room and headed towards the tanned colored leather couch she pointed out.

"No," I replied, sitting on the large couch and tracking the man's every move. He sat next to me on the couch, but not close enough for me to freak out.

The woman returned, sitting a bottle of water in front of me and one for her brother on the coffee table while she sipped from hers. She sat on the other side of me, closer to me than her brother.

Was I a fool to trust the way I felt around these two? I didn't feel threatened anymore. I sensed that they were protecting me based on our seating arrangement. I would venture to say these two took their job of safeguarding me seriously. *Like Primo said the loyal ones would*, the little voice in my head reminded me.

"What would you do if I called myself an Uber, got up, and left? If you're my protection like you say, don't you want me to feel safe, mentally as well as physically?"

Neither answered, but they didn't try to hide their smiles. Apparently, I amused them.

"I know this is a jarring situation to be in, but trust us on this, our family is in disorder right now, and you could easily end up in the hands of someone that would rip out your heart and mail it to Primo, just to get a reaction out of him," the sister said.

That statement shut me the hell up about leaving, for now.

Chapter Six

Primo

Regretfully, I stepped into the crowd, fighting a cringe with each uncaring bump that landed against me. My eyes were pinned on Nevah's retreating back while she approached the front door, thinking she was getting away from me.

My shoulders lifted high from an irritating sigh at the feel of my phone vibrating. I answered it despite the rowdy buzz of the crowd.

"You have eyes on you. Two, following," Brizio said. The ear piece I wore allowed his voice to come across above the noise.

"Head towards the bathroom. Trust me, they'll be stupid enough to follow you. I'll meet you there," he stated before clicking off.

"Fuck," I muttered, cursing this whole screwed up night. Nevah was the only bright spark to break through the darkness surrounding me, and she was darting through the front door in a mad dash to be rid of the likes of me.

Movement out of the corner of my right eye, gave me a glimpse at one of the men, dressed in a blazer and jeans in an attempt to blend in with the mixture of styles the club goers wore. If this was another attempt on my life, the notion of my hit being contracted to multiple killers was quickly becoming a fact.

My brow lifted in thought, wondering how much the contract was worth. How valuable was the price of my life to the requestor?

Thankfully, I had already put a plan in place for the new lady in my life. She still had no idea the situation she had easily stepped into would not be so easy to step away from.

As for the situation that was about to go down in the smaller of the two men's restrooms, I was fully capable and willing to dance with the types of devils that came looking for my kind of trouble. They didn't call me Hades for nothing. I would be in like company with whoever came for me.

The men blended into the crowd and although I didn't see them, I felt their eyes on me and sensed them closing the distance between us.

A devilish grin quirked my lips. There was no doubt in my mind that Brizio was already lurking in some dark corner thinking about the many ways he could manipulate death and unleash destruction.

Leading with my shoulder, I shoved the bathroom door open and stepped into the windowless space. Once the door closed behind me, the vibrating volume from the club was instantly shut out, plunging me into stilted silence. The area was larger than two standard bedrooms, more than enough room to set a few things straight.

The fact that Brizio had the area sound and bullet-proofed spoke for how often we'd had to handle some impromptu business.

At the sink, I pretended to wash my hands when the first man entered. This one wore a dark suit with expensive dress shoes. Based on his features, he was Italian. He glanced at me and dipped his head in greeting before stepping inside one of the four stalls without locking the door.

Ten seconds later, the second man opened the bathroom door, but he didn't enter right away. He turned and scanned the hallway for anyone who may have had eyes on him. Once he turned inside, he reached behind him and locked the door.

The man and his friend couldn't have been more obvious about their intentions. The one at the door took steps to approach me but snapped around when Brizio jerked the door open and stepped inside. I hadn't heard when the door was unlocked and apparently, neither did the man.

Brizio turned the lock once inside, and this time the metal gave off an ominous *click* that sounded throughout the space and made the man in front of me tense.

My gun was aimed at the head of the one who thought it was a good time to step out of the stall. Brizio aimed at the one who was angling to have a conversation with me at the sink.

"If you want to be recognized at your funerals, I suggest you toss those guns and tell us who the hell you work for," I commanded, my tone dripping enough acid to dissolve the air around us.

This was most definitely not The Malizioso and therefore had to be one of the families thinking they would catch us slipping in our own establishment.

The men complied with my command, removing their fingers from their triggers and lifting their weapons in surrender. Two guns *clinked* to the floor, one skittered over the slippery porcelain tile and stopped under the sink and the other slid under a stall away from its owner.

"Look, we don't want any trouble," Mr. Stall announced.

"Well it's too fucking late. You got it," Brizio stated, his tone hostile, edgy.

"We are just supposed to keep an eye on you and report it back to this number." Mr. Stall aimed a finger at his jacket indicating he needed to reach inside. I nodded, giving him permission to proceed.

A few seconds later, he produced a burner phone. Instead of tossing it to me, the man lunged forward with a superman punch that missed my face by an inch. The friend stupidly went at Brizio who rearranged his face when he palmed his gun to slap him with it.

The one fighting me made a quick upward attempt to launch another punch at my face, but I knocked it away hard enough to throw him off balance. With a quick spin, I gave my elbow the momentum it needed to disconnect his jawbone from his face. A sickening crunch sounded, ricocheting throughout the bathroom before he fell to the floor and howled like a wounded animal. The toe of my shoe caught the other side of his head, knocking that howl right out of his mouth.

"I'm quicker than I look, dumb ass," I muttered.

The man was so disoriented, he clawed at his jaw before he slapped a palm against it, attempting to hold his face together. His body teetered from the blows, his eyes heavy, glazed, and unfocused. His mind was halfway in another dimension while I stood over him, ready to knock his thoughts clean out of his brain.

The man in front of Brizio had taken up a defensive posture, his lip split wide open and the side of his face already swelling from the gun slap he received. With his gun now shoved down the back of his pants, Brizio eyed the man from head to toe and was calling him forward with subtle flicks of his fingers.

I shook my head. If arrogance was a person, Brizio was the poster child. The man, only feet away from him, was smart enough not to go one-on-one with him, most likely sensing my cousin's level of crazy.

My guy was still trying to figure out why he was on the bathroom floor. He held on to his lopsided face, his jaw shattered. I bent and reached for the burner phone he tossed at me and found one number programmed in it.

I tossed the phone to Brizio, who caught it over the shoulder of the man whose head was in danger of catching one of his bullets. He stopped his attempts to guild the man into a fight and retook his aim.

"Get that checked out," I told Brizio while he gave the phone a quick once over before nodding.

Brizio was my right hand and was plugged into so many networks, legal and illegal, that his alias count rivaled mine.

"Stand up," I barked at Mr. Stall. His memory appeared to be returning.

It took him several grunting tries, but he stood on wobbly legs, glaring at me with a look so hateful it would make the devil proud.

"Now," I said, tucking my gun into the waistband of my pants. "Who the fuck do you work for? If you need it in sign language, my man can help you out."

Brizio presented the man with a wide grin that flashed pure evil along with a sarcastic bow.

"We..." Mr. Stall sputtered, but I cut him off, lifting my hand and shaking my head. I saw the lie coming before he spoke it. Blood and saliva spilled from his mouth and hung in a long wet string down to his chest.

"I don't have time for bullshit. I've got bigger and better assassins out there waiting to take my life. You either tell me who sent you on a suicide mission or let us go on and get these two kills under our belt so we can move on with our night."

The one staring down the barrel of Brizio's gun shook his head, his face drenched in pity. "We don't know who hired us. We were wired the first payment and promised the rest if our intel helped lead to your death."

Based on the level of dread entwined in the man's words, he was more than likely telling the truth. Brizio nodded in my direction. He had a closer view of the man, and like me, had a knack for reading people.

"I hope you two have great life insurance," Brizio stated, his tone matter of fact and uncaring.

"You don't have to..."

Tap!

Bits and pieces of Mr. Stall painted part of the stall door behind him before his body landed in a dramatic trembling heap on the floor. The man's blood spatter had reached back far enough to paint one side of the face of his buddy. Whatever the man was about to say stalled as he tried to breathe and blink away the blood splatter that had gotten into his eyes.

"Damn Primo. You hardly gave him time to be terrorized," Brizio stated, his tone filled with amusement. His gaze lifted from the dying one on the floor and locked on the man with wide pleading eyes in front of him. The sight of his friend taking his last gurgling breaths while watching his own head contents motivated the man to beg harder for his life.

"I don't know who hired us, but I can find out. Please. I can find out for you," he promised.

I glanced at Brizio.

"I'm going to leave him in your caring hands. I need to figure out who sent The Malizioso after me."

I aimed my weapon for emphasis at the last one standing but kept my eyes on Brizio.

"These two are obviously not The Malizioso, but if you can, find out who sent them."

The smile on Brizio's face spoke to his demented state of mind.

"I got this Capo. You go and keep your date with destiny. I'll be in touch on this or that," he stated, never taking his eyes off his prey, but tapping the pocket in which he had placed the burner phone.

This man was going to pray that I had shot him versus his friend by the time Brizio was done with him. I was trained to kill by specialized professionals, yet I didn't get the kind of thrill out of it that I knew Brizio enjoyed.

I unlocked the door and for the third time tonight the noise of the club folded itself around me. Instead of The

Malizioso crossing my mind, it was Nevah who popped into my head.

My phone came alive in my pocket, calling my attention as soon as I traded the noise in the club for the silent night lurking outside the back of the club. My teeth grinded into each other, knowing the call would be more shit being added to the shit pile spilling over my life.

"Yes," I answered, not even bothering to see who the caller was. My vigilant gaze scanned my surroundings while I lurked in the darkness near a dumpster.

"Capo, Leandra definitely have eyes on her," Umberto updated. "We've been following the two who started trailing her vehicle. They followed her home and parked a few houses down to keep watch. You want us to find out who they are and handle them?"

I didn't miss the hint of enthusiasm in Umberto's tone. His or his brother Lenni's gun cocking in the background sounded. I was starting to believe my short reign as Capo had created some monsters who were more bloodthirsty and ten times deadlier than they had been two years ago. I hesitated a moment, thinking before I gave him an order.

"Whoever they are, they think Leandra is a soft target because she's a woman, not taking into account her last name. For now, watch the watchers. Don't engage them unless you believe her life is in immediate danger. They may lead you to whoever ordered them to watch her. The person that gives them orders is who we want."

"Understood," Umberto replied before hanging up.

Enemies were coming at us from every available angle. It made me wonder if there were more than two groups out there putting in requests for DeLuca blood.

**

"We have your *wife,* cousin. Picked her up attempting to hop into an Uber," my cousin Aurelio said. I could hear the tease in his tone over the phone line. I knew the moment I asked the twins to pick Nevah up and keep her safe they would not only have questions but would tease me since I was known for having a fuck-them-and-forget-them mentality where women were concerned.

"Thanks, Aurelio. You guys have perfect timing. I knew when I was speaking to her that she didn't believe a thing I was saying. Take her to S3, and I'll meet you there as soon as I can," I instructed.

The second call I made earlier tonight after The Malizioso had knocked me off the highway was to my cousins, Aurelio and Alesso, who, like me, knew how to deal with high-quality assassins. Although I knew they had their own shit to handle, they had dropped it to come to St. Louis to help me.

"No problem. We'll take good care of our new cousin-in-law," Aurelio teased before hanging up.

I couldn't help laughing but had faith that he and his sister would protect Nevah with their own lives simply because I asked.

Nevah needed protection after her brief encounter with me, whether she believed she did or not. A murderous coward in our family was roaming free and stirring up mayhem. The added stress left me unable to work at my full potential.

There weren't many people in the world I trusted enough to watch our backs, and the knowledge that two on my shortlist had arrived in the city in time to protect Nevah put a rare smile on my face.

Before taking on the Capo position, me and three other DeLucas were a part of a four-man team recruited by Don Ermanno himself.

The four of us were once the bastards of the family.

My mother and I were homeless for most of my young life, and I was abandoned to the streets of Sicily at eleven years old after my mother was killed by one of her Johns.

I was picked up by child protective services a few years later and placed in a home with a couple who abused me for years, physically and sexually. The woman used me for sex, and the man used me as his punching bag.

By the time Don Ermanno tracked me down at seventeen, both my foster parents' bodies were buried in their backyard, and I was living with and working for one of the toughest gangs in Sicily. Therefore, when I was approached, informed that I was a part of the DeLuca family and offered an opportunity, I didn't think twice about accepting the Don's offer.

He also recruited Alesso and Aurelio, twins whose mother had never disclosed who their father was, to prevent a scandal. Their mother having babies by a ranking member of the mob who was already married with a family would garner too much trouble and attention. The situation had marked the twins as bastards and outsiders until the Don offered them a name and a job.

Zaire was the fourth of us, abandoned at birth and brought up in a rundown orphanage on the outskirts of Sicily before he too was found and presented an offer. Don Ermanno's plan for assembling his secret team was brilliant, giving us all a powerful name and a purpose. He legally gave us the DeLuca name and a place within the family, even when the DeLuca men who sired us preferred to keep us their dirty little secrets.

A select few were aware that we worked for Don Ermanno on occasion, but they didn't know how in-depth those duties were. What would happen to our team now that Don Ermanno was gone? Had he shared our secret mission with Don Enzo, or would we have to eventually settle into our covert jobs within the family and let our secret operations fall into the shadows?

Whether the family knew it or not, our team was a necessary evil that prevented wars and started them if one was needed. Ultimately, we helped stabilize a deadly ecosystem built on death.

Each of us had agreed not to say anything about our extra duties unless the new Don approached us. If he never approached, we would take our secrets to the grave.

There were many secrets that died with Don Ermanno and unless I started digging up bodies and conducting blood tests, I'd never know for certain which DeLuca fathered me. From the history I'd uncovered so far, my mother had passed herself around to multiple DeLuca men back in the day.

Trusting the word of Don Ermanno was essential to keeping order. However, there were times when I got the sense that the DeLuca he revealed as my father, his dead cousin Eladio DeLuca, may not have been the truth. It could have been a convenient lie to save face with the family and to keep the bastard title off my head.

There were times when I caught Don Ermanno staring at me with an odd expression like he wanted to say something, but he never did. There were times when I wondered if I had any DeLuca blood running through my veins at all, and it was that very thought that kept my curiosity about my father at bay.

With a hit out on me, I'd had to swallow my pride and call for the kind of backup that was on the same level as the hitmen after me. The twins, Aurelio, male, and Alesso, female, home station was located in California. Although Alesso's home base was in Cali with her twin, her code name was "The Traveler" due to her executing hits in over thirty states so far.

It had taken them a few hours to arrive in St. Louis since they were laying some groundwork for the past few weeks for a mission they would soon start in Chicago. I was set at ease knowing that they would be protecting Nevah.

Now, I needed to shake this tail I picked up outside of the club. Killers were swarming, anxious to cut the cord on my lifeline, but as time went on, I had become more eager for the fight. They were poking a savage, and I planned to give them every bit of demented energy that raced through my blood.

My way of handling the enemy was usually quiet, but always deadly. I poured a lot of time, money, and energy into keeping a low profile, so this was the most popular I'd ever been in my life and career.

I drove Brizio's silver Dodge Challenger, cruising along Grand Boulevard and allowing my tail to creep closer so I could pick up clues about them.

The idea of multiple groups gunning for me was a compliment to my reputation.

Chapter Seven

Primo

A selenite gray Mercedes S600 was what I made out. The Malizioso would use every trick in the book to not appear suspicious. Therefore, it astonished me that I had spotted them so easily.

I cruised until the crush of the city started to thin, bobbing my head to the nonexistent tunes bumping in the car.

My loft sat at the edge of the city a few miles before the sturdy foundations of expensive subdivision homes revealed the exquisite masonry work it had taken to create them.

The sound of the tires crushing the crumbs of loose pebbles on the asphalt sounded when I turned into my driveway. The short expanse led me down to the garage and basement level.

Once I stopped at the steepest part of the decline, I reached out and punched a code in the small black box on the wall to spring open my garage door. The building was meant for two occupants, but I owned both apartments which were replicas of each other.

The second apartment was a decoy registered to a tenant who didn't exist. The building was reserved for special occasions like the one I would soon be engaged in tonight.

I hopped out of my car with a keen sense of purpose. The danger in the air was so thick it clung to my skin and seeped into me with every breath I took. I keyed in the code to the back entrance and took the stairs to the second-level loft area.

I flipped on the lights to set the mood of a man who was in for the night. A few seconds of quick maneuvering allowed me to enter the adjacent loft apartment through a special door cut between the coat closets.

In these spaces, there was no need for any lights. I knew every inch of the building like the back of my hand because I'd spent months staging and memorizing every detail. This space was fully automated, reacting to my voice, my fingerprint, and retinal scan.

I keyed in the numbers to open the state-of-the-art surveillance room to see how many assassins the infamous group had sent on their first attempt to kill me. How would they make their approach? Multiple screens gave me a view of everything inside and outside the building, including the roof of those beside and adjacent to mine.

While waiting, I threw on my protective gear and armed myself with a few handguns, extra ammo, a few knives, and sat my rifle within reach. I slid my cell from my back pocket, dialed, and held it against my ear with my shoulder while operating the surveillance equipment.

Alesso answered before the ringtone sounded on her end.

"Hello."

"How's my lady?"

I didn't have empathy for many things in my life but was finding that I had it in abundance for Nevah. She had been dealt an unfair hand tonight, but what was done was done.

"She's begging us to let her go one minute and threatening to walk right out the door the next. She's feisty. I like her." Alesso snickered, and I could sense her eyes were on Nevah while saying it. "I explained that this is a tumultuous time in our family and not safe for her to be unprotected. I believe she understands, but she's still having a hard time accepting her new position. She'll come around. It just hasn't sunk all the way in yet."

"Okay. Take good care of her until I get there. I've got to go," I said, eyeballing the two pitch-black motorcycles rolling up to the building across the street. I zoomed the camera in, waiting to see what they would do, but they sat in place, unmoving.

Instincts made me check every camera and angle. It was a good thing that I did. The bikers were decoys, stationed there to distract me while others crept in through the back door of my building, the area I preferred receiving my guests.

The Malizioso were paying me a compliment by sending at least six of their men to try and take me out. However, it would be their loss because I had something special for each one of them. They didn't call me "Hades" for nothing.

Inside the same coat closet that gave me access to the spare apartment was a trap door in the ceiling. I stepped in, closed myself inside, and climbed up. To cover my tracks, the door was automatic, and when it closed, the area below it became lined again with my old sweaters and jackets.

The confined space I was currently crawling through had small monitors at every turn, allowing me to see a smaller version of what was displayed on the screens inside my surveillance room.

The first floor and second floor loft level above it was set up for living with custom-designed furniture, each piece equipped with its own special surprise. I waited in the far corner of the ceiling above the couch in my upper level loft. My feet hung over the drop behind the wall that would feed me down to level one and further into the basement.

The first two killers were set to enter through the kitchen and sweep the lower level. Their lips moved as they sprung the lock, entered and began their search for me. They were radioing updates back to their friends.

I waited, observing a second team of two entering through the thick back door off the garage. This area led to the foyer that would lead them up to second level and loft.

The teams were good at their jobs so far. Their technique of covering each other while one overrode the door locks was above average. They didn't walk right into the foyer but cracked the door open and entered as a team with their silenced guns covering all directions after they stepped inside.

It was a nice solid B performance. Personally, I expected more from The Malizioso, but every group had its weak spots.

They scanned the area, remaining soundless and not flipping on any additional lights. They were equipped with all the good stuff—body armor, night gear, and laser sights on their weapons. Despite their reinforcements, I had rigged this place to be an inescapable obstacle. There was no amount of high-tech gear that was going to help them out of the brutal mess they had stepped into when they entered my house.

The team of bikers sitting out front hadn't moved an inch. However, another pair were scaling the wall and heading to the roof, where there was a way in through the skylight. They were welcomed into my sanctuary of the damned.

The team rappelled in through the skylight, sliding down a thin rope that lowered them into the loft's living room. My eyes flicked to the camera that showed me the first team. They were sweeping the first level living room like members of a SWAT team.

As soon as the feet of the two rappelling from the skylight hit the floor, their bodies started to jerk violently, like they were doing a high-impact version of the hokey-pokey. Clenched teeth, gaping eyes, and spasming bodies, they looked a mess.

The rubber soled boots they wore weren't enough to ground them from the charge. The space around them was an electrical field. Their bodies collapsed into a heap on the charged floor, popping from the electricity coursing through them.

The two inching up the steps to the second level were smart enough to stop in their tracks at the high-pitched yells and frantic thumps their electrified friends' made, disrupting the quiet. They eyeballed each other, thinking twice about proceeding any further.

One of the two on the first level living room had his hand up to his ear, receiving or replying to a message. Soon after, the team spun with caution, their weapons moving fast and securely up and down while they searched for the danger they knew lurked.

The overwhelming scent of burning hair and skin assaulted my nose and polluted my lungs with every pull of my breath. The remaining four continued their search. I watched one on the lower-level inch closer to the X marking the spot I saw through the special blacklight lens of the camera.

"One more inch," I mumbled under my breath, smiling because the man's feet danced near the mark.

"Aww!" he yelled when the floor fell from beneath his feet, and gravity sucked him down to the basement level right into my special prison cell.

The one left on the first level and the final two who entered the second level loft proceeded with caution. It was too late for caution. When they entered the loft and saw their baked friends, I'm sure they reached the same conclusion.

I headed for the basement, sliding down the chute that landed me face to face with the frantic man pacing inside the cell. The side of his head was busted and bleeding, a gift from the fall he'd taken. He'd managed to keep a hold of his gun, so he lifted it and fired off three rounds. The bullets bounced off the clear bulletproof wall of glass in front of me.

"You son of a bitch! Let me out of here," he growled before firing off a few additional rounds. The floor he stood on hummed when I flipped the switch that turned on the magnetic pull inside the cell. The polarizing force jerked his weapon from his hands, leaving his mouth hanging open. The bulge under his shirt protruded, indicating that his belt was caught in the pull of the magnet before I turned it off.

"Now that we're better acquainted, why don't you tell me who hired you?"

Based on the devilish gleam in his eyes, I was certain he wouldn't give me an answer. A smirk spread across his lips, letting me know that he was unaware of how much hell he was about to pay whether he gave me an answer or not.

"The room you're in is fully contained, which means anything can happen to you in there, and no one outside this room would be the wiser."

He contemplated my words, his eyes aimed up in thought. The sound of me flipping another switch got his attention.

The floor was lined with burners, spewing flames that shot up about a half foot high. The heat licked at his feet and ankles, making him dance around uselessly. I wanted to see him try and climb those glass walls.

His eyes were as wide as silver dollars. Now that I had gotten his attention, I turned the fire off, enjoying the way he continued to hop around like a tiptoeing, hot-footed thief.

"Who hired you?"

A goosebump-inducing scream sounded from above, followed by a barrage of curse words. The others had found out by now that the only way they were leaving my house was in a body bag.

My question hadn't been answered by the one glaring at me with a look that had the potency to kill. The sight prompted me to flip the switch again so I could enjoy my daily dose of entertainment. This man's knee lifts were of the caliber of a fitness instructor.

"Let me out of here, you fucking sick freak! I don't know who hired me. It's not like they did a face-to-face interview."

"Tell me something I want to hear," I said, observing the way the heat melted the skin of his boots and cooked his feet. He wasn't screaming yet, but his pain level was written in the deep creases of his face and his tightly gritted teeth. I'd turned the fire off, but the *swish* of sprayers followed and captured his full attention before they started spitting accelerant onto his pant leg.

His head rocked back and forth so quickly I expected his vertebrae to snap.

"Don't do this shit, man! You can't be that fucking evil!"

"This coming from the man who broke into my house with five others and your biker friends out front, each with intentions of torturing me before you took my life," I pointed out before folding my arms across my chest. Despite his erratic movement, I managed to see the question among the fear flashing in his gaze.

I was in the same business as he was and knew damn well they would torture me before killing me. My position within my family meant that I was a book of secrets they wanted nothing more than to crack open.

"It's business. That's it. I don't know who hired me," he whined, his voice high-pitched.

"See, that's the fucking problem with half-assed hitmen. You don't take the proper time you need to study your target or invest in finding out who hired you. It's all about the money for you these fucking days."

The below average behavior of this group of hitmen was beginning to piss me off because I was wasting a perfectly good setup on them, and it would take weeks to restore my apartment.

"What happened to the good old-fashioned art of studying a target so intensely, you end up knowing them better than the people who knew and loved them? What happened to the days when you became so good at your job that getting caught was next to impossible unless you wanted to be caught? You're not an amateur. But now that I'm up close and personal with you, I can clearly see that you're not The Malizioso, either. Right?"

He shook his head. "No."

"Pretending to be The Malizioso to throw me off is an insult to me and to that organization. You had to know I'd figure out you guys were pretending to be one of the deadliest death squads on the planet."

He was too busy staring down at how wet his legs had gotten with accelerant to pay attention anymore.

I tapped the tip of my pistol to the side of my head in thought before I glanced up and met his pleading gaze. My hand rested on the switch that would ignite the fire and give this man a taste of hell on earth.

"Man, please! Don't do this," he whimpered. Fear had his legs trembling and his right eye twitching.

"Give me something." I put pressure on the finger I kept against the switch, making him fold into his shoulders.

"I overheard some of the guys," he gritted out. "They think the person who hired us was a DeLuca."

I hadn't expected him to say anything, and the fact that he did, had me thinking about the state of the hitman society. The bit of information about who may have hired them got my hackles up and confirmed my suspicions.

"We're the middlemen, contractors. This shit is bigger than us. Once you're gone, there are plans to take out more DeLucas, if necessary."

My icy gaze locked on his shifting eyes, protruding from the sockets. "You see, that's the fucking problem. You all are assuming that I will be killed."

His face pinched, and I noticed the moment the impact of his hellish surroundings crushed the last bit of hope he foolishly clung to. He could have been mouthing off untruths to stir up more turmoil since his time was dwindling. Or there very well could've been someone out there with an ego the size of Texas who actually thought they were about to execute me and more DeLucas.

"Who the fuck are you? We're usually hired one or two at a time, but never twenty of us for one person."

Another secret revealed that let me know exactly how prepared I needed to be. I pressed my face closer to the glass so that he could get a good look into my eyes.

"I'm Primo. Your fucking beginning and your end. The only way I'm dying is when I get tired of running shit up here and decide it's time to go and run shit the right way down there in hell."

At those words, it appeared he'd swallowed a boulder. A smirk that I knew mirrored pure evil sat on my lips.

"None of you are going to get past me for the chance to take out another DeLuca. The person who hired you could have sent a hundred, and I would kill you all just to feed my ferocious appetite for the taste of death."

His body deflated at the notion that he would die soon. His wide gaze lifted from the area where my hand rested on the switch to meet my eyes.

I flashed a smirk before I flipped the switch and walked away without even a glance back. His screams were the legendary stuff that gave a hitman a temporary high.

The strangled cries of the caught and the damned met me when I climbed out of the wall's secret passage and walked into the open space of the loft. This was where the second team of two had ventured to and ended up fucked up.

One man was dangling from the ceiling, caught in my razor wire net. It had been activated after he'd stepped atop the camouflage netting that matched the flooring. The razor wire embedded in the net's thick, hairy strings whispered the man's fate into death's ears.

He was on his stomach with his legs jacked up in the netting. His body weight and positioning had his face and the front of his body wet and red with blood.

His eyes were wide with enough fear shining in them that I read his unwillingness to move even a centimeter. His blood dripped to the ceramic floor tiles, tapping out an ominous beat from the multiple areas he leaked from.

The floor below him resembled a sadistic blood-splatter painting.

A low chuckle escaped after I spotted his buddy.

"I see you've been introduced to my version of a glue trap."

He had backed into a wall of glue, the consistency thick enough for a quarter of his body to be embedded within the thick wall of death. He sunk deeper with every move. Even his fingers were trapped where he'd tried to break free.

His large eyes followed my movements when I stepped closer, and the pleading in them was easily conveyed. With a flip of a switch, the square trap he was stuck in shifted about half a foot back.

"Let's see if we can get you all closed up and cozy."

The front of the trap was a mirror to the back. When it began dropping down on top of him from the ceiling, the man yelled, his voice projecting the fear he couldn't express through movement. He was set up to be encased in a sticky situation, so hellish that I almost felt sorry for him. On second thought, it wasn't sorrow, but reluctance at the knowledge that I'd miss out on his expression when he suffocated.

A peek at the monitors showed the bikers still in place outside the building, clueless that their friends weren't succeeding at their tasks. Their motorcycles nearly blended into the shadows of the front of the building near a tight alleyway. The moonlight reflected off the exposed portions of their pale skin. With them in the crosshairs of my rifle's scope now, I moved my aim back and forth between them.

"Eeny, meeny, miny, moe," I sang. "One of you is going to die while the other runs and alerts the other guys."

I squeezed the trigger, and the head of the one sitting on the right and nearest to the alleyway exploded. I watched his body tumble off of his bike and drop to the ground like an empty suit falling from a hanger. The dark swallowed his body and hid the gory details of his final portrait from passersby.

His friend jumped from his motorcycle to take cover, scrambling on his hands and knees. He peeked in every direction, unaware that he remained in my kill zone. A fucking shame. The hitman community was turning to shit. Was I the last of a dying breed?

I slowed my trek through the first floor living room at the sight of the one who'd gotten impaled by the harpoon I'd rigged to go off when he opened the door to the hall leading to the bedrooms. His partner was in the basement, well-done. None of the men had made it any further than my living rooms.

It was time to call for house cleaning. I snatched up the keys to my bike, not wanting to leave in the same vehicle or go in the same direction I had arrived.

"Hello," came the calming voice on the other end of the line after I dialed.

"I have a big job for you. The scene is still hot so wait until it cools off."

"Understood," was all my cleaner said before hanging up.

The remains in the basement were smoldering when I passed them on my way to the underground passage that would lead me to the other side of the building. A quick check of the monitors didn't show any immediate threats.

My bike's engine hummed in anticipation of being revved when I drove along the driveway on the opposite side of the building. I was a nightmare waiting to happen, carrying an impressive array of weapons strapped on various parts of my body.

The drive to the safe house was a peaceful one, allowing me time to think about Nevah and how my life impacted hers. I was a wanted man and always would be, which meant she would inherit my danger.

Knowing I was no good for her, why the hell was I thinking of ways to incorporate her into my life and not making plans to send her back to hers? Sending her back to her life would inevitably happen, and I'd do it, but right now, I rejected the idea of never seeing her again.

The short time that I was in her presence, we had hardly exchanged words, but it didn't stop a sense of knowing from taking up residence in my psyche. All I wanted to do was protect her. Now that I was on the verge of seeing her again, I would get the opportunity to figure out if our connection was a one-time fluke or if there was something more to us.

Chapter Eight

Primo

I lifted my face to the camera at the front door so the twins would see me clearly. The door popped open, and a weird need to see and touch Nevah again made my pulse race. I tempered my steps, feigning a calm and easy stride that didn't match the anxious edge riding me.

The living room sat empty, but the sound of the television in the den drew me in that direction. Aurelio and Alesso acknowledged me with head nods and wide smiles, that said more than words ever could.

Alesso, with her small frame and delicate features, had an approachable demeanor. Aurelio, with his brawny size and towering height, appeared the more intimidating of the twins. However, Alesso was older by ten minutes and the most dangerous of the two. Thankfully, the twins weren't the hugging kind, so our head gestures and smiles sufficed for greetings.

Nevah sat with her legs tucked under her and her head against the back of the couch facing Alesso, and Aurelio sat behind her. My cousins might have appeared like two normal people to outside eyes, but upon seeing the way they surrounded Nevah, I saw two of the deadliest assassins I knew protecting my precious package. One would never know that, like me, they were carrying enough weapons on them to take out a ten-block radius.

Nevah's head lifted when I stepped closer to the couch. The moment her eyes met mine, they grew wide with recognition. She stood quickly and appeared to be preparing herself to run.

She rushed in my direction with a quiet sense of relief washing over her features. When she threw her arms around me, tight and sure, I released a little chuckle at the action.

This situation didn't make any logical sense. We didn't *know* each other, but it felt like we *knew* each other.

"You okay?" I asked, whispering into her hair after wrapping her in a tight embrace. A deep inhale gave me a good whiff of her alluring scent. My hands were rubbing up and down her back with a caring touch I didn't even know I was capable of delivering.

She glanced up, locking those big brown eyes with mine.

"I'm scared. I want to go home."

Her tone rang with sorrow and a quiet pleading that made me want to fulfill her request, but I couldn't. And although I suspected that she was scared, I wasn't picking up fear.

"You're my responsibility now. I can't let you go off alone and end up hurt or killed."

My words had tears welling up in her eyes. I couldn't imagine how she felt and prayed, one of those emotions was confidence in me and my ability to take care of her. My arms tightened around her, folding her in a reassuring embrace.

"I won't let anything happen to you."

Her head dropped and rested against my shoulder before she nodded, acknowledging my words. The throat clearing ceremony taking place drew my attention. The twins stared at me with Nevah like they were seeing a marvel in the making, their brows pinched tight with confusion.

"Nevah said that you two met tonight. It certainly doesn't appear that way," Aurelio stated, his eyes narrowing at the sight of us.

"Is there something you want to tell us?" Alesso questioned, continuing where her brother left off.

"No. We met, we're here, and now we have to figure out how to live with how we got here," I said, being vague on purpose. I couldn't explain how we had gotten here anymore than I could explain my weird attraction to Nevah. All I knew was that I wasn't willing to allow the person who was after me to get to her.

"It was a DeLuca who ordered my hit, and I don't think it's meant for only me. Someone may know what *we* truly are. If so, *we* may be a part of the hit that took out Don Ermanno. Either that or there's another DeLuca here in St. Louis that is out for DeLuca blood."

Nevah's head jerked up, her gaze flashing around the room at each of us before she placed it on mine.

"You weren't lying at the club. Your own family is really trying to kill you?"

"Yes," was all I said. I wanted to say more but reminded myself that we were only hours into our relationship, and I'd already said too much in front of her.

"We're going to give you guys some privacy. I need to get some sleep," Alesso announced, her gaze bouncing between me and Nevah, who hadn't let go of me yet. The quick thump of her heartbeat pumped fast and strong enough to tap out a beautiful rhythm against me. She was scared, and I was the only thread of safety in this world that was unknown to her.

I cast a quick nod at each of my cousins before they stood and left the room, their steps in sync. The rhythm of their footsteps faded before their doors closing sounded. I walked us to the couch and sat with Nevah tucked into my side, her head resting against my pec.

We didn't speak one word but sat comfortably within the security of our embrace. Her gaze fell to my right hand, taking in my missing digits for the first time. She retracted the arm she had around my waist and moved it closer to my hand, not stopping until her fingertips were brushing mine.

My first instinct was to jerk my hand away, but the idea that she was willing to touch what some people found disturbing was impressive and endeared me to her that much more. She kept her hand atop mine and melted into my embrace without saying a word. Her action caused a smile of contentment to settle on my lips for a long time.

I hadn't realized I'd fallen asleep until my head made an attempt to detach itself from my neck. Nevah was lying on her side with her head on my lap. Her mouth was so close to the bulge in my pants, it appeared she was preparing to give me head. The sight made me harder and forced me to reposition her in an attempt to calm down.

Once I placed a small pillow under her head and covered her with the throw from the back of the couch, I let my head fall back. The ceiling was the perfect blank canvas that allowed me to think clearly about all that had taken place tonight.

***

My gun was up, aimed, and ready to fire before my eyes had fully opened.

"Put that away," Alesso said in a low tone, unbothered that my gun was pointed at her head. Her gaze dropped to Nevah, whose head was in my lap atop the pillow, except she had managed to wrap her arms around my torso. Her breaths were low and labored, revealing that she was fully asleep and perfectly comfortable.

Alesso's smile widened, and she finally lifted her gaze to meet mine. "Never thought I'd see the day," she whispered. "But I guess it happens to the best of us."

My brow lifted in response to her comment while I tucked my pistol back under the pillow next to me.

"Aurelio is staying. I'm going to join Zaire in Italy so we can work this thing from both sides of the planet."

I nodded, knowing we had answers to find before the DeLuca family tree lost more branches and leaves. Alesso cast one more glance at Nevah and met my waiting gaze once more before she walked away, shaking her head and grinning.

Chapter Nine

Primo

"I'll eventually be able to return to work, but what about my mom? I visit her at least once a week."

Though she'd needed time to accept it fully, Nevah was much calmer now about her situation.

"Hopefully, we'll have a resolution within a week or two. I'll make sure someone checks on your mother and reports back to us until you can resume your normal schedule. I also need you to take some DTO days off from work and stay away from your friends and family."

She nodded before releasing a giggle.

"They are called PTO days. Paid Time Off."

I nodded. "Yeah. Well, I meant DeLuca Time Off. You can call the days whatever you like but take them off. You could probably use a break anyway."

Another giggle. I was beginning to enjoy the sound.

"I've only taken time off a few times in the three years that I've been at the hospital. I always manage to do everything I need to on my scheduled days off. What am I supposed to do with all this time, knowing that I can't go anywhere?"

Her question was low and unsure. Still processing her current situation, she was questioning herself for an answer more than she was me.

"I have a few safe places you can go. I can send you and your mother away and hire a caregiver to take care of her needs."

The horde of questions she wanted to ask were visible in the tiny creases around her forehead and eyes.

"You would do that for us?"

"You're my responsibility now, and I'm a man who takes his responsibilities seriously."

She held her tight expression, thinking. "You're being hunted. You're a mob boss. I have enough common sense to know that things can get *dicey*. But I don't want to uproot my mother or run unless it's absolutely necessary."

At the club, it appeared she'd wanted nothing to do with me when she found out who I was and about my situation. Now, a surreal sense of calm seemed to have washed over her.

"Why not take the easy route that I'm offering?"

Her shoulders lifted in a slow shrug. "I don't know the fine details about your world, but I understand enough to know that no place is truly safe. I'd rather stay close to you."

The glint of conviction in her eyes confirmed that she already had an unshakable belief in me, one I rarely saw in someone I'd just met. She trusted me to protect her.

"Being near me is the most dangerous place you could be or one of the safest, depending on how you look at it," I stated truthfully.

"I don't care. It feels safer than me being off some-place wondering if the mob has found me and is preparing to put a bullet in my brain. I'll take my chances with you."

I handed her a disposable phone. "I have to work on figuring out who has a hit out on me, as well as assist in finding out who put the hit out on our late Don. It could be the same person. The sooner we figure it out, it will be safer for us all." I paused, feeling the need to add a clause to the declaration. "As safe as one could be in our world."

She handed me her palm without protest when I stood and reached out for it. We walked hand in hand until we reached the kitchen pantry. Once we were inside, I placed her hand between the third and fourth shelves of the seven stocked nearly to the ceiling with canned goods. I pushed her hand past the cans until it touched the slight dip in the wall.

"Spread your palm and push hard," I instructed.

Her eyes grew wide before she placed her free hand over her mouth at the sight of the shelves spreading apart. The hidden doorway behind the shelves shifted open with a low pop.

"If you get a sense that danger is near, I want you to come here."

She glanced back and forth between the wall and me. A step took me close enough to shove the door further open before casting a head gesture back at her to follow me.

We descended the stairs leading to the small, base-ment-level safe room that only I knew about. She entered the small seven-by-ten room with slow choppy steps.

Her wide eyes scanned, the setup leaving her with parted lips. The space contained a state-of-the-art surveillance station, a well-stocked, open-faced weapons closet, and a tan couch shoved against the back wall.

"You have a safe room inside of a safe house. Is there *that* much danger in your family?"

"Depends on who you ask. My day-to-day operations as Capo are not as dangerous as what I can otherwise encounter. Let's just say, I do more for my family than they will ever know."

She didn't reply, but there was a sense of knowing in her penetrating glint like she was figuring out something in her head.

"Aurelio and Alesso weren't exactly hiding that they were hunting people down for your family. I believe they trusted me to a certain point, because of you. I know that you're the leader in this city. Based on what you said about the possibility of the family traitor having an idea of who you guys *truly* were, I got the impression that the three of you have a separate agenda outside of what you do for your family and disclose to them."

"You would make a good little detective," I complimented, unable to help grinning at her.

"Can I ask you something, and you give me an honest answer?" she asked, looking at me from eyes that now held reluctance.

"I haven't nor will I ever lie to you about anything."

She flashed me a cute, crooked smile before dropping her gaze. Whatever she wanted to ask dealt with a heavy subject because she wasn't a shy person based on what I knew of her so far.

"Will you kill me if I become someone who's not worth the trouble or if I get in the way?"

It bothered me that she felt the need to ask me the question, but I sensed it wasn't because she felt threatened by my presence. She wanted assurances on her protection.

"Like I mentioned to you earlier, women are off limits. So are children. It's a rule we follow in this family, emphatically. There are ways we can punish you without inflicting bodily harm or causing death. However, if we promise to protect you, we will do it even at the cost of our own life."

She folded her lips into a tight knot, fighting a smile, but unable to keep it from shining in her eyes. She liked my answer.

"I appreciate your answer. But shouldn't it be a crime for you to insist on my involvement with *you?* Your life revolves around danger and death and adding me to the mix automatically makes me a target."

"You make a good point that I have considered multiple times. However, you have to also consider that you could have been killed a thousand different ways leaving your house this morning. Being around me might be dangerous, but death will come when it's ready, no matter your situation."

At that statement, the room grew silent, and the noise of our steady breaths came alive. The light crinkle around her eyes disappeared before she inhaled and released on a long, steady breath.

She was still in the process of putting order to our situation in her head. I was done with the reasoning behind it all. She had grown on me already, and in addition to procuring her safety from the murderous spy in my family, I'd already decided that I wanted her *for good.*

"Always remember this," I said, recalling something I needed her to know. "If you're ever in earshot of me, and I start a countdown. I need you to do whatever you need to do to get down, get out of whatever path you may be in, or run like hell because someone is more than likely about to die or something is about to blow up."

She nodded and her unblinking eyes lifted in thought.

"Nevah," I called, my tone low, my gaze locked and pouring into her.

"Yes," she answered, her brows pinched.

"Three. Two. One…"

Her eyes twitched before recognition flashed in them. She let herself drop to the floor and assumed a prone position, covering her head with her arms.

A big grin broke out over my face, wide enough to make my cheeks ache. I was never more proud of anyone than I was of this woman at this moment. I bent to help her up, the smile on my face greeting her when she looked up and grasped the hand I offered.

"You are a woman after my heart," I told her. "You listen to me, better than some of my men," I complimented.

The sight of the smile I put on her face did strange things to my damn insides. I ignored the urge to rub my chest all of a sudden and focused on adding to her self-protection portfolio that I prayed she would never have to use.

A crash course on how to operate the surveillance equipment followed, allowing her to see a 360-degree view of the house's exterior and of various rooms inside the house. I proceeded to instruct her on how to lock herself inside the safe room while pretending not to feel the effect she had on me.

Chapter Ten

Primo

Once Nevah had received her lessons in self-preservation, I gave her a quick tour of the rest of the house before making the final stop at our bedroom.

"Are we staying there together?" A furrow creased her brows.

"Yes. Death may be unpredictable, but if it comes knocking, I prefer that it be me who answers."

"Oh," she said, allowing her gaze to travel around the room although she hadn't moved to step inside.

"I enjoy being labeled a savage, but I've never, nor will I ever cross the line you're thinking about right now."

She flashed a twisted smile.

"You're wrong about what you think I was thinking."

"How so?"

"I was thinking that it's been a long time since I've been in bed with a man. I was wondering if I wanted to be a good girl or a bad one."

The blood in my veins ran hot before a substantial amount traveled south. Next thing I knew, my hands were sliding around her waist before I drew her to me, making our bodies kiss.

"Please, don't be good. Be bad. Be very bad," I whispered before I lowered my lips to hers. The first soft caress of our swirling kiss closed my eyes, her pillowy lips melting into mine. The calming warmth, the supple caresses, and the little whimpers that slid out of her mouth and vibrated into mine fanned the heat of the passion burning through me.

My intention was to not go there with her this fast, but that damned statement of hers had opened the freeway of impure thoughts I'd been having about her since I'd first laid eyes on her.

Now, I needed to show her why I staked my claim before anyone else could get their hands on her. If she was playing a brilliant mind game on me and was one of the assassins, she would have to wait until after we were done before she executed her attempt on my life.

My tongue slipped between her lush lips, and she deepened the kiss, sucking so hungrily the sparks of our passion threatened to burn me alive. The fumes from the blaze shot straight to my already hard dick.

Fuck.

Her body was the epitome of sexy, her tits full and supple, and her plump ass felt good in my hands, even through her jeans.

I had taken more time vetting a woman I was planning to fuck in a bar bathroom than I had Nevah. However, none had captured my attention so fully and instantly. She made me forget about that dark part of me that craved certain aspects of death that would earn me the label of sociopath.

I didn't have a name for it yet, but Nevah was special and so fucking sexy that the mere sight of her made me forget myself. She had a unique way in which she held my stare, like she could shimmy her way into my thoughts and take control of them. And her body...

"Shit," I growled, filling my palm with one of her tits while the other went sliding over a plump ass cheek.

Reluctantly, I drew away from our kiss, loving that sex-crazed glint in her eyes. She was as ready as I was, her body jittery with edgy movements that acted as the voice for her arousal.

"This doesn't make any sense." She whispered the words like they were a secret. Her face was a mix of confusion and lust. "I hope you don't think I'm normally like this, jumping on every man who lays claim and disguises it as a rescue. But you..." Her hand flicked along my abs before she sat them in place, undecided on her next move. "There is something about you that my body and mind craves, no matter how crazy the circumstances."

My lips brushed her forehead. The delicate kiss was an unfamiliar sentiment on my part, but I believed she needed the reassurance that she would be okay. That we would be okay.

"That's one of the best compliments I think I've ever received from anyone. You might as well go on and propose to me," I suggested, offering a lopsided smile while my hands rested at her waist.

The comment had her leaning back and glancing up with a teasing side-eye.

"Don't look at me that way. You know as well as I do that something is going on between us. I don't know you,

Nevah, but I know that I want you in my life and that it would be extremely difficult for me to let you go."

She didn't reply but threw her arms around me in a hug so tight, it was like she was using the snug embrace to stave off the charged energy consuming us. I couldn't explain us any more than I could predict the weather.

The strength of the hug affected me and brought on a surge of weird impulses, but it wasn't all sexual. The emotional charge expanded and dragged me out of the fog of my lust. It allowed me to absorb the unique and all-consuming connection we were sharing.

This was a first for me. We stood there, held within each other's embrace. I rested in the peace, quiet, and comfort that settled over us.

Her body rested heavy against mine before she stepped back and out of my hold. Based on the alarming expression creasing her face, I believe our connection scared her. I didn't protest when she turned and headed for the bathroom, casting a quick glance back in my direction before closing the door softly behind her.

The spray of the shower sounded, and I remained in place for a long time. My sexual urge, and I suspected hers as well, had faded into the background. How was that even possible? All I wanted each time she allowed me to see her vulnerability was to make her feel safe and to know that I cared about her feelings. All else, even my sexual urges, became secondary to my desire to comfort and protect her.

***

A while later, I returned to our bedroom and found her in our bed. The sight of her in my too-big clothes was a pleasant one. The fact that she hadn't asked to use them was an unspoken statement I didn't know how to decipher yet.

She sat with the covers pulled up to the bottom of her knees. My shorts were so long on her that I only peeked a small brown glimpse of what I knew were sexy legs. I'd washed up in one of the spare bathrooms and thrown on a pair of black basketball shorts and a plain white T-shirt while she was getting her bathroom therapy.

"Feel better?"

"Yes," she said, scanning my every move as I approached and climbed into bed.

"Tell me it's going to get better, Primo."

She came into my embrace willingly when I lifted my arm to her.

"It's going to get better. I promise. We just happened to meet at a difficult time while the DeLuca family is in a state of mourning and transition. Therefore, wolves are going to descend, and we are going to defend and protect this family even if the wolf we need to put down is a part of it."

She nodded against my chest while cuddling closer against me. There was something about this woman that put a spark of therapeutic excitement in me, a new smooth flow to the jagged one I owned. When her body rested heavily against mine, indicating she'd fallen asleep, I moved us down into the covers and relaxed into the state of perpetual peace surrounding us.

Chapter Eleven

Primo

The sound of my phone buzzing at six in the morning wasn't unusual. The phone waking me up early had never bothered me until this moment, with Nevah lying in her rightful place on my chest.

Dammit!

The last thing I wanted to do was leave her alone, but duty called. I placed a delicate kiss on her forehead and cheek and eased from beneath her. She released a low whimper before settling her head into the pillow.

"Yeah," I called into the phone when I was out of earshot. It was Brizio.

"Calling cousin Aurelio to the city has paid off. His behind-the-scenes-working-ass wouldn't let me help him, even after I practically begged. I'm sure, by now, there's a trail of dead bodies all over this city and possibly state, but he managed to find us a lead as to who put the hit out on you."

Brizio was a creature of the night, so at six in the morning with darkness still flirting with the moon, he was bursting with enough energy that I could feel it through the phone.

"Aurelio's hunt led to a low-level member of the Vittorio family, who I found whispering about mingling with an enemy that would soon be taken out. I didn't know if Aurelio found a way to put him right under our noses, but guess where I found him?"

It wasn't a question, and I could tell from the glee in his tone that Brizio was enjoying this hunt we were executing.

"His dumb ass had the nerve to be sitting in *my* fucking club while talking shit. I ran the surveillance to figure out what he was saying. Needless to say, I have his grimy ass in my basement." He paused, and I swore a low moan sounded. "I damaged him *a little* for the shit he was talking about, but so far, I haven't been able to get any more out of him."

"I'm on the way. Don't *damage* him to the point that he can't tell me what I need to know."

"Okay," he said, his words rushing out after a loud *thump* was followed by the man I informed him not to damage, yelling out in pain.

Brizio had a mean streak in him that few knew about. He showed people what they needed to see to have a good time while he studied and siphoned information from them the whole time.

After one last peek at Nevah and taping a note to the bedroom door, I locked the house down. I hated treating her like a prisoner but was unwilling to risk her being harmed because of my current situation.

***

By 6:35 a.m., I stepped into my cousin's club for the second time within a twelve-hour window. The floor was littered with discarded paper, empty glasses and bottles of wine, and trash was on every surface.

The place smelled like a mix of hyped-up testosterone and heat-seeking pheromones. If you stood in place long enough to analyze the scents, you could distinguish perfume from cologne, body odor from body aroma, cigarette smoke from weed smoke, and much more.

"Capo," Brizio called while I was taking the final few steps into his secured basement. It doubled as a sex dungeon and torture chamber, one I had used to conduct business as often as him.

When I turned the corner, I was brought up short. There were two men, each tied up from head to foot and dangling from a thick metal pipe like pigs on a spit. All that was missing was the apple in their mouths.

"Brizio?"

"Meet Creto Vittorio and the crooked federal agent he was in my club with."

A smile spread slowly across my lips, giving life to the sparks of joy coursing through me. The feds always had the kind of information we were searching for and were the first to spill their guts when pressure was put on them.

I bent, getting face to face with Creto. His family was mainly based out of New York, but he worked for one of the Vittorio family operations that was run out of Kansas City, Missouri, about three and a half hours away and on the opposite side of the state. The temptation of the DeLuca family's success often brought spies, and some over the years had been dumb enough to poach in our territory.

"Why are you in my city, Creto? You know better. I stay out of your business, and you stay the fuck out of mine, and we'll never have a problem. However, you being here means we have a big fucking problem, especially when there's a squad of hitmen aiming to take my life. Did your family hire them?"

"I came here to meet with a contact that invited me," he said, glancing at the agent.

"Okay, but that doesn't explain why you were in *this* club with said contact while two groups tried to take me out. What the fuck are you up to? What would your family gain by allowing you to breach our territory, not to mention you mouthing off about a member of the DeLuca family on the verge of being taken out while you're inside of a DeLuca establishment?"

"I was talking shit." His face squinted in a mix of confusion and fear. "How could you possibly know what I said?"

Brizio read lips and body language like a bibliophile raced through good books, but I didn't answer Creto's question.

"We don't have any beef with you crazy-ass DeLucas. I wouldn't have shown up if I wasn't invited here by one of you."

Creto denying what he was truly up to was pissing me off. I extracted a metal ball from my suit pocket and twisted it until it glowed to life. The sight of the little sphere, with its blinking red light in my hand, had the agent shaking his head with fear-widened eyes. Even

Creto was smart enough to stop talking and pay attention to the little jawbreaker pinched between my fingers.

I turned, my black Ferragamos scraping the floor as I inched closer to the begging agent. My dress etiquette was an element of my personality that had been inspired by Don Ermanno. As a result, I rarely went anywhere without dressing in a full suit.

"No!" the agent yelled out, his head shaking so vigorously, spittle flew from the corners of his lips.

"Don't come near me with that thing. I only feed the family inside information about cases that may cause them problems and the occasional scraps of information we've gathered on your family."

I believed he was speaking the truth. Was he aware that he'd admitted to feeding our enemy information the feds had gathered on my family? Did he know he'd verbally signed his own death certificate?

"Why were you in a DeLuca club?" I dragged each word of the question out since they were hard of hearing.

"I already told you. We were invited," Creto sputtered, his eyes fixed on the little metal ball I was lifting towards the agent's mouth.

"If you were invited, who the fuck invited you?"

"I don't know, but they claimed they wanted to discuss business."

"Sounds like a fucking lie to me," Brizio stated, rolling his eyes at Creto. There was no doubt in my mind that Aurelio had found a way to entice these two idiots into the club. A part of our training had been learning to pimp a lie into a convincing truth.

The agent shook his head like his life depended on it to keep me from shoving the sphere into his mouth. His desperate movements forced me to put a knee in his chest to control him long enough to shove the ball into his mouth. A few of his teeth cracked during the process. The sound caused Creto's wide eyes to grow bigger.

Brizio was kind enough to hand me a piece of packing tape to keep my little toy inside the agent's mouth. My cousin was nothing if he wasn't efficient. Who was I kidding? My cousin was an undercover sadist who somehow managed to find people who begged to be tortured at his hands. Therefore, watching me scare the shit out of these two was a little thrill for him.

If Brizio thought I didn't hear the scratching and muffled groans of whoever else he had tied up down here in his dungeon of sin, he was crazy. I didn't even bother asking. The sad thing is, I didn't know if it was someone who had volunteered to be down here or not. However, pretending not to hear the sounds seemed to add to the amount of fear pouring into Creto and the agent's hearts.

I dragged the agent up into a sitting position before instructing him to slide closer to Creto. The man's mumbling words were almost understandable, him begging me not to proceed with what was rolling through my savage mind.

I reached back to my cousin for the roll of tape while keeping my eyes, one of them twitching, on the begging men. The agent continued his muffled cries while Creto had no shame in mouthing the word "please" repeatedly.

My phone rang.

"Yeah," I answered, keeping my dead eyes set on Creto's fear-drenched ones. A smile crept across my lips at the update.

Creto wanted to know what I was being told so badly, I could feel the anxiousness rolling through him and pouring from his begging eyes. I swiped my phone off and shoved it into my jacket's inner pocket without taking my eyes off Creto. My quiet stare was driving him nuts with the way he chewed into his lip and the rapid movement of his shaking legs.

"Come on, Primo. You know I didn't mean any harm. My family has nothing to do with this hit that's out on you."

"You're lying. I have it on good authority that the men who came after me worked for your family. Imagine that? A whole damned squad of twenty. What I can't understand is, why? Even if you take me out, I already have a replacement. And trust me, I made sure he is just as, if not more vicious than me."

"I don't have anything to do with the hit that's out on you. I do what I'm told, and I was told to come here and meet with our CI," he said, glancing at the man who continued to mutter sounds around the tape over his mouth.

"Your father is doing the right thing, making you work your way up, but you're the nephew of a Don. Neither he nor your father is going to send you into the belly of the beast without a reason or without protection."

His eyes grew wide at the revelation, like it was rocket science I'd figured out.

I extracted another sphere from my pocket, and although Creto didn't seem a worthy adversary due to his blotchy skin and flabby body, he fought harder than the fit agent to keep me away from his mouth. However, I forced the sphere inside and slapped a piece of tape over it before taking a step back to admire the beginning of my handiwork.

"We found your protection detail," I informed Creto, peeling more tape from the roll. Brizio stepped up and shoved the two men's heads together, producing a fleshy smack. With their cheeks kissing, I taped their heads together, leaving them each one eye for visibility. Impairing their vision was a way to make their situation that much more intense.

Brizio roped them together so tightly, they hardly had any wiggle room to breathe. He also assisted me in loading the men after I dragged a dolly closer.

We rolled them down the dark hall, through the underground passage out of the club, and to Brizio's van. Muffled cries and two pleading eyes were all the men had in their favor while we pushed the dolly up the ramp and shoved the two into the back of Brizio's van.

"I'll follow you," I told Brizio. He nodded, stepped around the side of the van, and climbed into the driver's seat, whistling the tune, *Whistle while you work.*

The sun had long ago painted light across the darkness, allowing the day to emerge. The warm July wind blowing against my face helped awaken my mind to clearer thoughts. I didn't doubt the Vittorio family had other spies out there keeping tabs on us, the same way we kept tabs on them and any other family we'd had beef with in the past.

What I couldn't understand was why Creto would be dumb enough to come into a DeLuca establishment even if someone had invited him. Did he have that much faith in his protection detail? Or did he have that much fate in their hired guns ability to take me out?

Chapter Twelve

Primo

The roar of my motorcycle idled when I turned onto the service road that led to a private quay sitting on the Mississippi River. We drove along an alley next to a line of warehouses sitting off the pier.

The Vittorios had purchased the warehouse a few years ago, thinking they were being sneaky. They were unaware that we were the ones who sold them the place. It was located in neutral territory but gave us insight into the Vittorios' activities.

The tin that covered the outside of the warehouse was speckled with rust, the remaining paint flaking off the building like dead patches of skin. A large section of the roof was missing too, giving the building the appearance of being abandoned.

I followed Brizio inside through a large opening in the side wall that appeared to have been ripped open by an angry DeLuca. A metal fence rolled to a squeaky close behind us, securing the opening. We drove deep into the building until we reached a large portion rebuilt for the illegal gambling operation the crew often ran from this location.

We parked, and a few of our guys gave a wave before assisting Brizio with transporting our captives. The muted cries of the two men echoed through the dusty and drafty space. Brizio carted them through the building like they were slabs of slaughtered livestock.

"Capo," Bartolo called out, and judging by the way he'd said my title, he wanted a word.

He greeted me with a head nod and accepted mine in return. The way our men were running around the warehouse, you'd have thought it was still ours.

Bartolo leaned closer to me when I stepped in front of him. "Aurelio caught the two who thought they were following you here. He said they put up a fight and lost the battle before he could extract any useful information."

"Okay, appreciate the update," I said before stepping off. Someone wanted me dead and was willing to lose a lot of men attempting to accomplish the mission.

The doors to the offices on either side of the long and wide hallway in the back of the warehouse were left wide open. Brizio had beaten me to the office and was standing outside the door. Distressed voices emanated from within. His twisted smile was one I knew well. It had that savage twinge to it that let me know he was down for whatever evil deeds sprouted from my brain.

I stepped into the office, noticing the furniture inside was shoved against the wall to my left. To my right was an old metal desk missing one of its skinny legs and shoved against the other wall.

Four men from Creto's ten-man protection detail were lined up against the far wall directly in front of me. They were being guarded by my cousins Angelo and

Lucca, each with automatic weapons aimed and primed to shed blood. Machetes rested against their backs, anchored in place by thick black straps.

They were two of our newest to become made. At twenty-two and twenty-three, they had put in the work and proven their loyalty enough that I was keeping an eye on them for a few special projects I had in store for the future.

It didn't take but a glance at our prisoners for my brows to shoot up in recognition. Two were higher-ranking members of the Vittorio family. Creto's cousin, Prevlo, who was next in line for Capo of Kansas City, and his Uncle Genovio were also among the crew. This was too much family power to be Creto's protection. What the fuck were these Vittorios up to?

Brizio abruptly stepped out of the office, pulling all of the attention. He returned, wheeling in Creto and the agent so that the four sets of swollen and bloodshot eyes watching could see that whatever Creto and the agent had been up to in St. Louis had failed.

The human cargo was parked in the center of the room. The scent of blood, sweat, and fear permeated the air, an odor I was used to breathing. I stood next to the bound men, staring down the line of the ones against the wall and finding two brave enough to meet my eyes. Silently, I assessed and stalked them with my gaze, allowing them time to get their lies in order.

"Anyone mind telling me who was stupid enough to stir up the fires of hell and *try* to take out a DeLuca in his own territory?"

Brizio took a seat on the wobbly desk, facing the men with his feet dangling over the side. He'd withdrawn a pack of peanuts from his pocket and was casually popping them into his mouth like he was watching a movie.

"No one has anything to say. Well, let's see if I can get you guys talking."

I drew my weapon, aimed it around the room, and stopped on Creto before I pulled the trigger. Cries of protest on Creto's behalf sounded.

Creto's groans, though muffled, still managed to ring with enough anguish to fill the thick air with more tension and send a vibrating tingle through me. I loved the sound of the damned.

"I aimed for his leg the first time, but I promise you, the next bullet will be in his fucking head if you don't tell me something. Are you willing to stand there in your silence and let me start a war, one that you all can't, and won't win? Why the fuck are so many of you in St. Louis? Did you come to make sure I was dead? Who hired the team of hitmen to take me out?"

Wide eyes, a few open mouths, and faces masked in seriousness, stared. It was only a matter of time before one cracked.

"An answer to each question would be nice."

Eyes traveled back and forth between me and the shivering Creto. Tears dripped from his one visible eye while he muttered unintelligible words.

"Bit of advice. If each one of you gives me a partial answer to each question, it doesn't count as snitching."

Two sets of brows lifted, considering my proposal.

"We were assigned to protect Creto," the first one stated and received accusing eyes from the rest. However, when I placed the barrel of my pistol to the back of Creto's head, another began to mutter a few words.

"Speak up. I can't hear you."

"We're not always informed of why we're protecting someone," he said, letting me know that Creto may have had answers that they didn't.

I pointed at Prevlo. "You're next in line for Capo. If anybody knows anything, it's you. Talk, or he dies. Don't talk, and you all die. Don't fucking matter to me."

He shook his head, eyeing Creto with a sorrowful glance when I pressed my pistol deeper into the back of his head.

"We are not the ones you should be interrogating," the first who'd talked, muttered. The ones talking were the reason most low levels didn't mature to "made" status.

The tape prevented Creto from talking, but in his state, I was willing to bet he would sing like a fucking canary. It was too bad his current situation couldn't be undone.

"It wasn't disclosed to us who hired the hitmen or why, but a DeLuca set this in motion," the first who had spoken grumbled the statement and lowered his eyes to avoid the deadly gazes he knew were cast on him.

The comment confirmed that although they didn't know all the details, my hit was being carried out by the Vittorio family and brokered by a fucking DeLuca. At the admission, Prevlo and Genovio held the murderous glances they shot in the talker's direction.

Satisfied with the new information, I stepped back and joined Brizio near the desk, pretending I was analyzing them for more questioning. I'd likely gotten all I would get verbally, and although I wanted the DeLuca they were stupid enough to work with, they had given me more than enough to indulge in the depraved fantasy swimming around in my head.

"You." I pointed at Prevlo. "Un-tape your cousin and this agent bozo. I'm interested to see what they have to say."

The taped men began mumbling and struggling so hard against the ropes binding them, veins popped out on their necks and the visible parts of their foreheads. Their bodies jerked with a frantic need that made the dolly under them move.

Prevlo took a step, his movement hesitant, his eyes curiously set on how the men squirmed and attempted to communicate with him.

"This is about to be good," Brizio muttered, staring at the beginning of the un-taping in rapt anticipation. He was enjoying this scene more than me. I was a monster, had no tolerance for bullshit, and Brizio knew it. He rarely got the chance to sit in on my sessions, and when he did, he didn't leave until the party ended.

The top layer of tape came off, taking hair with it. Prevlo stopped unwrapping to cast a glance at me. He sensed that something was wrong, but he didn't understand that the men he was unwrapping were doing a good job of shaking their heads and muttering what *I* understood were the words, *"No!"* and *"Stop!"*

Instead of paying more attention to Creto and the agent, Prevlo kept glancing in my direction. If he was waiting for a hint from me, he was about to experience what infinity felt like.

Brizio never dropped his eyes away from the un-taping. "Should I take cover?" His tone was low, but his voice oozed excitement.

"No. Sit tight. I'm interested in knowing what's about to happen myself."

I sensed the eyes of the men against the wall on me but didn't give them an ounce of my attention.

"Wait, what?" Brizio asked.

Prevlo ripped off the second layer of tape, yanking out more hair with his unwrapping method. Once the men's heads were separated, Creto was able to spit muffled words out around his wet tape.

"No, don't remove the tape!"

However, his words were a second too late.

The agent's mumbling rants became frantic, the sound racing from his gut and roaring past his throat only to become trapped in his mouth. Prevlo snatched the tape free.

As soon as the agent's lips were pulled apart and the sphere was exposed to air, his head exploded. Chunks of seared meat, brain matter, and blood particles flew about three feet into the air. Cerebral content landed at mine and Brizio's feet as sprinkles of blood and internal matter dotted our clothes.

The force from the blast lifted Prevlo and threw him back about five feet before he landed on his ass. Angelo, Lucca, and the men on the wall had all taken cover, but the fireworks weren't done.

When the dust settled, Creto wobbled his way to a standing position before stumbling closer to the line of men who stared like he was a monster who'd broken out of hell. An apple-sized chunk of the top of his head had splattered over the floor, and brain matter and fluids slid down the side of his damaged head.

He wobbled closer to the men, making them slink away with protective hands covering their faces. His animated head and twitching body continued dragging along like that of a reanimated corpse. Whatever was left upstairs acted on the impulses that remained. He stumbled, and a deep wobble sent him falling at his uncle's feet.

Genovio stood above his fallen nephew with his eyebrows scrunched tight. His lips were pinched in seething anger while silently murdering me with his penetrating glare.

I folded my arms across my chest and kept my eyes glued to the uncle's. "Got anything you want to say? Who is the DeLuca you're working with?"

As expected, he didn't answer and had no intention of doing so. He knew this life, knew that no one in this room would survive. Not even the building would survive after what had happened to Creto and the agent.

I pressed my finger to my earpiece to get the attention of the rest of the DeLucas scattered throughout the warehouse.

"Men," I called in an authoritative tone, my gaze locked on the older man's. "Top to bottom, every office, room, and closet. If you find anything to do with my hit, namely who else and which DeLuca might be involved, I want to know about it."

Brizio's crazy ass stood above the half-headed agent and observed the damage the small bomb had made.

"You're a fucking homicidal lunatic," he stated with an actual smile on his face.

Angelo and Lucca left the men on the wall to assist with the search party. The remaining men sat nursing the extreme amount of anxious energy coursing through them. I sat deathly still and studied them like they were specimens under a microscope to see if they would give any type of sign that would reveal when we were close to finding answers.

Brizio worked on a laptop belonging to one of the damned, scanning it for any information or clues on how the Vittorios had linked up with a rat ass DeLuca to put a major hit out on me.

Three hours later, the search continued.

I clicked on my earpiece. "Tell the men to take a lunch break and come back in an hour."

It was Bartolo who responded with a simple, "Yes, Capo."

***

Six hours later, a meal of St. Louis style pizza the men brought me around five p.m., and we still hadn't found one thing that linked the traitorous DeLuca to the Vittorio family. It could have been part of the family's plan to turn us against each other for all we knew.

"I've got something," my cousin Bartolo called out before crossing the threshold to enter the office. He stopped short at the sight of the headless agent lying in a pool of his own blood. His brows lifted at the sight of Creto slumped in the corner he'd staggered into, a chunk of his head missing. The toxic mix of blood, shit, and piss strong enough to water the eyes and trigger the gag reflex pooled at his feet.

Bartolo shook his head at the scene and absently handed me two pieces of paper. "I think you'll want to see this."

He continued to survey the horrific scene, eyeballed the dead men, and wrinkled his nose at the scent of expelled bodily fluids permeating the air. A quick glance showed me what was handwritten on the stationery bearing the DeLuca seal.

One of us had handed the information to the Vittorio family. In the world of digital technology, the Vittorio family was about to lose some members over a handwritten note they'd been too lazy or too arrogant to believe they needed to destroy.

Brizio walked up, and I handed the pages to him before I approached the remaining men on the wall.

Pop!

Pop!

A bullet was delivered with my blessing to each of the snitches' heads.

"Shit!" Genovio murmured, wiping blood from the side of his face and staring with a glare mean enough to cause physical damage.

"Holy fuck," Brizio called out at the sight of the mess I'd made of the men, particularly the one whose leg spasmed although his body had fallen and landed in the prone position.

My phone vibrated and a quick peek showed that it was Nevah calling. The sight of her name appearing on my phone had me forcing down a smile. Just like that, she'd pulled me out of the savage haze I'd allowed myself to sank into. The phone was up to my ear before I noticed what I was doing. I'd never taken a personal call from anyone while I was putting in work.

"Hello."

"Primo," her quiet tone sounded, and I'd never been so grateful to hear someone's voice.

The list that Bartolo had handed me was a list of the DeLuca safe houses. A few of the houses weren't known to all DeLucas, which meant the list of potential rats had been narrowed down to about thirty versus a hundred. The house that Nevah currently resided in wasn't on the list, but my need to protect her was stronger than ever.

"Nevah, I need you to listen and listen well. I want you to go down to the safe room and lock yourself inside."

Her voice cracked. "I can't."

"Nevah?"

My heartrate kicked up a notch.

"Your black Barbie doll has my best friend aimed at the back of her head," a male voice threatened. "Now, *I* need *you* to listen and listen well. Come alone..." the voice said in a threatening tone, mimicking some of the words I had just spoken to Nevah.

"Come alone. Any extra DeLucas, and this lovely woman is going to find out why it's not a good idea to date a man in the mob."

He paused and the silence had me thinking he'd hung up until his irritating voice returned.

"By the way, you have impeccable taste in women."

The dial tone screamed in my ear.

Fuck!

"Brizio…"

"I've got this," he called out, although he eyed me for more information on what my phone call was about.

"Nevah," I whispered, not wanting anyone else to know that more drama was brewing. Brizio's lips pursed, and although he tried to hide it, I saw pity flash in his gaze.

"Can I kill the last two?" Brizio called his question to my back as I was marching out.

"Destroy everything living and inanimate," I replied without so much as a backwards glance.

The Vittorios had killed as many of our men, so our killings should count for the life-for-a-life code that most mob families lived by. Not to mention they had breached our territory to witness an assassination attempt on me that they had facilitated.

They had allowed their egos to lead them through the gates of hell, assuming the low-key attitude I practiced as Capo of St. Louis meant that I was soft. They were unaware that I had perfected the art of lingering in the background, speaking with few words, and asserting my authority without spotlighting myself.

If the Vittorios wanted a war after all the violations they committed, they had awoken a beast that was ready to deliver gifts shipped straight from hell. However, the worst act they had committed wasn't the hit they initiated on me or breaching our territory to watch me die. The worst thing they did to me was put their fucking hands on Nevah.

I promised her that I would keep her safe, and in less than two days my promise was being broken, and a fucking gun was being aimed at the back of her head.

Chapter Thirteen

Nevah

Earlier.

I rolled over, shaking the haze of sleep with ease while encircled in the quiet warmth of expensive bedding. An explosive sex scene hadn't occurred between Primo and me last night, but oddly, a sense of satisfaction coursed through me like we had sealed the deal.

The memories were vivid and sweet, and Primo was so intoxicatingly male that it was difficult to believe I'd fallen asleep on *him*. His smooth, spicy scent lingered on the sheets and on me like the invisible particles had found a way to seep into my skin.

My first instinct was to reach out for him, although I had caught a glimpse of him tiptoeing out of the room earlier. He was danger personified based on what little I knew about him, but the way he treated me, like I was the most precious thing he'd ever had in his life had me wanting to glue myself to the man.

The realization that he was also partially responsible for blowing up my life screamed a noisy reminder like a siren going off in my head. On the one hand, he'd saved me, and on the other hand, he'd trapped me. This gorgeous house and all these gorgeous things surrounding me made this a beautiful prison.

The way his *cousins* had so easily dragged me off the streets, and the pep talks they gave me about their family's enemy was enough to scare me straight. Common sense also kept me in place since I had no desire to face whoever was out there gunning for Primo.

I was thirty and although I'd had trouble nailing down a decent man, I still desperately wanted what I'd never had growing up—a family. Since my dreams of marrying and having kids hadn't happened yet, I had to be cautious, especially in this world where death loitered on every corner.

After forcing my body from the cushiony comfort of the mattress, I rolled to the edge of the large California king bed and tossed my legs over the side. The smooth fabric of the large rug the bed sat atop tickled my toes and brushed smooth strokes to the bottoms of my feet.

Why couldn't he have been a painter or even a lawyer? Primo was a ranking member of a crime family, a made man, and a secret hitman on the side. It was best to keep reminding myself of those highlights before I foolishly gave myself permission to do the one thing I had no business doing—falling for him.

Jesus!

I stood and began my trek across the room, admiring the clean splendor of my surroundings while I approached the bathroom. After relieving myself and a quick hand wash, I used the toiletries I found last night, brushing my teeth and freshening up. The massaging spray of the dual shower heads had lured me back to a peaceful state of mind and given me a touch of heaven.

I moisturized and wrapped myself in a towel before entering the bedroom on a mission to find something to wear. The knowledge that I was without clothes was another reminder of how quickly my life had been turned upside down. I'd have to find something in his closet until I washed and dried the clothes I'd worn to the club last night.

When I flipped the lights on inside Primo's closet, the sight of it stopped me in my tracks. The neatness. The suits. Many expensive ones. All of them black. The only differences were in the shades of black and the patterns of the material.

"What is his fascination with black?"

My fingers brushed a dark blue long-sleeved button-up before taking it down. I picked up a silver and black pin-striped tie from his tie-rack that I used for a belt and made myself a shirt dress.

I was shit-out-of-luck in the underwear department.

Now what?

I roamed the room, being nosy, and discovered his note taped to the door informing me to make myself at home. I snooped the rest of the house including the three other bedrooms. None were as well equipped as the room Primo and I were occupying.

Once in the kitchen, I found the refrigerator fully stocked and proceeded to make myself some scrambled eggs, fruit, and toast with black coffee after I figured out how to work the coffee maker and insert the K-cup.

After I was done with breakfast and cleaning the kitchen, I washed my clothes, hung my blouse to air dry, and tossed the rest in the dryer. I was used to waking up to a set schedule of work and daily tasks, so this silence was threatening to strangle me. Like now, I would have been at the hospital making my rounds.

Hours later, after occupying myself with lunch, I binged on Netflix. Periodically, I paused the show to peek whenever I heard a sound outside, hoping it was Primo.

Before I could panic about my phone being missing, I found it along with the disposable Primo had given me sitting on one of the two end tables next to the couch. The first thing I saw on my phone was a text from Tracy letting me know that she and Maya had made it home safe and sound. I texted her back.

"Good, now would you please advise our girl to take a class, on class *like I've been suggesting?"*

The phone pinged before I could set it down.

"Class is overrated. Same time next week? We gotta find you a man."

I paused, my fingers lingering above my keys, unsure how to respond. *If she only knew.*

Before I could feed her a bullshit line, a key jiggling in the door's lock sounded.

Primo!

He had left when there was still a touch of darkness in the sky this morning, and now night was starting to settle in once more. The prospect of seeing him had me up and on my feet, ready to meet him at the door.

What was it about this dangerous man that drew me in like this? I was practically bubbling with excitement and couldn't for the life of me stop myself from walking closer to that door.

His warnings about being careful while he wasn't around knocked me in the head, and I stopped dead in my tracks. What if it wasn't him at the door?

Instincts controlled my feet, and cautious steps edged me back. Why was it taking the person so long to get the door open when a simple turn of the key should have done the trick?

The door sprang open, and I jumped so hard, I gripped my chest to keep my heart from popping out and hitting the floor. There was no one there, but I continued taking shaky steps back as my breaths flew out fast and hard. When I managed to get my legs to turn me in the opposite direction, a male voice that wasn't Primo's commanded, "Don't move."

The urge to run like hell had my body pulled so tight my muscles ached and the biting tension swarming around me threatened to open up a gaping hole to swallow me. I feared moving, that even an inch would be the last move I made.

The little hairs on the back of my neck that stood when danger was near were doing their job, but they were about a minute too late. Who the hell was behind me? How had they gotten into the house so easily without triggering the alarm?

Light steps drew the person closer, sharpening the edge of my anxiety. The sound of their breathing behind me registered before the cold metal butt of a pistol pressed into the back of my skull.

"Do what I say, and you will survive this."

The hard edge to such a gently spoken sentence made me shiver before my legs threatened to give out.

Chapter Fourteen

Primo

Nevah.

Her name was a constant echo inside my head, each chant reminding me that time was a monster gnawing at every thread of calm and logic I possessed. Every second, every minute, every breath I took represented a mark in time that she was under a killer's gun.

He wanted me to come alone. He was going to get me too: signed, sealed, and delivered. The devilish twitch in my eyes and the edgy tremors of rage racing through me represented the exact version of me he was about to receive. If be-careful-what-you-wish-for were a person, my picture would turn up.

Why the fuck did I think it was okay to leave Nevah alone at such a tumultuous time? She'd been alone from sunrise to sunset, more than enough time for someone to hatch a plan.

She was an innocent civilian who wanted a normal life. If she ended up hurt or killed, it would be on me, and it wasn't something I was sure I could handle. I was getting her out of this shit if it was the last thing I did with my life.

The hundred-plus miles per hour wind whipping against my helmet and the world blurring into swirling colors in my peripheral vision didn't faze me. The bike's tires sounded like a squealing pig due to my aggressive driving.

Finally, I reached my destination and ditched the bike in thick shrubs a few houses down from my safe house. I towed off my shoes and jumped my neighbor's fence before trekking through the only blind spot from the cameras in my backyard. The living room lights were visible outside the house through an opening in the thick curtains that gave me a peek at the moving shadows through the thinner drapes.

My phone, now linked to my earpiece, buzzed. The action told me my early arrival wasn't anticipated.

"Hello."

"You should be arriving soon. Try anything funny, and I would hate to make this beautiful woman cease to exist."

"I'll be there in a few minutes," I told him while opening the secret cache of weapons I'd stashed in the backyard inside the deck's steps.

"How do you want to play this? You're expecting me to walk through my front door and let you shoot me?"

"You in exchange for the lady," he directed.

What kind of dumb ass was I dealing with? Did he actually believe that I was about to walk into that house and let him kill the both of us?

"*Fucking idiot,*" I mouthed while climbing atop the neighbor's pool house roof.

"I'm walking up to the house now," I lied while inching across the top of the building to find the perfect spot that would allow me to see into my living room.

Foolishly, he had drawn the thick top layer of curtains open, thinking he would see me approaching through the sheer drapes. Instead, the thin drapes gave me enough of a view to see his profile standing behind Nevah, who was sitting in a chair. Although their images were blurred, I could definitely see that he was aiming a weapon at her head.

Knock. Knock. Knock.

"Come in!" the man called, adjusting his aim at the back of Nevah's head. He'd fallen for a pre-recording of knocking, playing from inside the house. *Dumb ass.*

I had a contingency plan for a contingency plan and had hundreds of actions and commands recorded and stored in the house's automation system. Being prepared in this business kept me alive on many occasions.

"Before I step through this door, let me speak to Nevah."

Finally, I'd found the perfect spot to stage my rifle to aim at the asshole holding my woman hostage. The problem, she was in the line of fire too.

"Come in, DeLuca. I don't have time for any of your fucking games," he mouthed, shaking the weapon at Nevah's head.

She was silent, no begging or even whimpering. I wasn't sure if there were tears, but she was thankfully not overreacting.

"Let me talk to her before I place myself in your deadly path," I demanded.

He released an irritated sigh before lowering the phone closer to her mouth.

"Nevah, are you okay?"

"I'm scared, Primo. Are you coming to get me?" Her voice wasn't shaky. It sounded strong.

"I'm here. I made you a promise that I wasn't going to let anything happen to you. Do you remember what we talked about *right* before I showed you how to work the surveillance equipment in the safe room?"

"Yes," she replied.

"Tre! Due! Uno!" I counted down in Italian before seeing her jerk sharply down and out of the man's reach. He scrambled to retake control of her.

Good girl.

One flex of my finger on my rifle's trigger, and the asshole dropped like a sack of stones. A loud scratch sounded from the phone hitting the floor, but the line remained open.

"Shit," I heard Nevah say. "Primo, if you can hear me, I think they have someone else hiding outside," she yelled, and I could hear her running, her feet tapping out a thundering beat. She was running towards the panic room, and she hadn't left the phone behind.

That's my girl.

Within seconds, the one who was hiding revealed his position, creeping out of the shrubs near the fence. His intention had been to shoot me in the back while I approached the front door.

I patiently held my position and waited until he was creeping across the living room floor. He stood above his dead friend and glanced around like an idiot before I blessed him with one of my devastating kill shots.

Clinging to the shadows, I hopped back across my neighbor's fence, grabbed my shoes, and dashed into my backyard. Once inside the house, I crept along the dark hallway and snuck a peek into the living room at my handiwork. I avoided any area that could be seen from outside the house in case they'd been smart enough to have one more lookout.

I used my phone to tap into the intercom inside the safe room.

"Nevah, it's me coming down."

"O..." she said, lifting her finger from the button too soon and cutting off the rest of her word.

I cracked the pantry door open, stepped down, and typed in the pin to pop the safe room open. Nevah tackled me before I made it past the threshold.

"Primo," she cried, cuddling her face into my chest. I squeezed her in a tight hug, kissing the top of her hair.

"I apologize for allowing my world to sneak up on you like this."

She glanced up, eyes glistening with unshed tears and her face surprisingly calm despite her body's coiled tension. Those big, pretty eyes were a weakness I was finally admitting to myself.

"Life as I knew it is gone, isn't it?" she asked.

"Yes, sweetheart, it is. And I apologize for that, but it won't always be this way."

She didn't answer, but the emptiness filling her gaze bothered me. I didn't want this life for her, but I didn't have anything else to offer other than me and protection.

"Let's get out of here."

She nodded. "Yes. Please. This time, I go where you go. I don't care where it might be. What scares me even more than dying, is dying tragically and alone."

"I don't think—"

"No," she cut me off. "I stay with you, or I just as well walk out into freeway traffic. What if the next one rapes and tortures me?"

Her words prompted unsavory images of her beautiful flesh bloodied and scarred. The notion of it had me ready to kill someone who didn't exist.

"Okay. You stay with me. But I must warn you; I don't run from trouble. I hunt it down and bless it with a solution."

She swallowed and stared at me like I was the dark shadow standing above a freshly dug grave. Her thinking gaze remained on mine, searing into the depths of me for answers I still couldn't give, until she pointed a finger at her chest.

"I'm not as green as I may appear. I grew up in a neighborhood nicknamed, *The Grind* in the Sunset Heights housing projects. I scratched, clawed, and worked my ass off to get out of there. I've seen dead bodies. I've seen people killed. I've slept under my bed at night to avoid a stray bullet. I know how it feels to live life under the gun. I know hunger and neglect. But, I don't want to die a horrible death alone and for no other reason than being in the wrong place at the wrong time."

I noticed right away when she'd said the wrong place and time, but not the wrong person. The sentiment embedded in her words, even if she didn't realize it, meant the world to me. She was inadvertently cementing herself to me. We were never going our separate ways if I had anything to do with it.

The projects she'd grown up in bore a certain level of fame for the amount of danger and death they produced. It also bore the name, "The Walking Graveyard," because children had about a 50/50 chance of making it to adulthood. Based on where she grew up, she understood this life better than I could have imagined.

Her upbringing may have prepared her for the street life, but was she ready for me? I wasn't ready to show her who I was outside of who she currently saw me as, but life had plans other than the ones I made that would allow her to see all my sides.

Chapter Fifteen

Primo

Nevah jumped into the clothes she had worn the previous night after pulling them from the dryer. We took the alternative route out of the safe house before we trekked back to my bike.

She clung to me so tightly that not even the noisy roar of the motorcycle's engine or its endless vibrations kept me from the vibrant energy transfer she gave off. It was the same energy that made me lay claim to her in the middle of a DeLuca meeting.

Thirty minutes later, we ditched the bike for my gray Nissan Sentra that I kept parked in a hotel's parking garage. The car slowed, my foot easing from the gas by the time my thinking caught up with my actions.

We were closer to the city this time, right on the edge before the population grew dense and the surroundings became too busy. This location was the least likely place anyone would search—a trailer park.

I stayed in the trailer periodically, a place where no one was the wiser about my identity. It was my retreat of sorts, the place I went when I needed to think and strategize. Nevah looked around, turning in her seat to scope out the location. She had surprised me with her request to stay by my side versus distancing from me for safety.

The fumes I was running on had burned out, leaving my raging mind to fall out of sync with my exhausted body. I glimpsed our surroundings, taking in the scene before hopping out of the vehicle and walking around it to help Nevah exit. For now, we needed to brave the storm we were caught in, and if we made it through, it would be the test that proved we were strong enough to be together.

Once I unlocked the front door, I opened it and allowed her to step inside first. I had purchased the two-bedroom mobile home and moved it to this specific park because it sat in a nook away from the high traffic and denser populated areas. My older neighbor, Mrs. Benton, who believed I worked as an offshore rigger, was happy to make the extra money I gave her to keep the place tidy and stocked.

"I promise that I can afford better for you. But, right now, this is probably the safest place we could be."

"This is actually nice and cozy. It has a homey vibe about it that is more welcoming than that huge safe house was," she said while continuing to take in the place. "After what just happened at the house, I get it. I'd stay in a tent in the woods if it means I live to see another day. The terror I just experienced was the kind of scare that makes you appreciate life and puts in perspective how much and how often we take it for granted. In the grand scheme of the last day and a half, this is perfectly fine."

Pride swelled my chest. There weren't many people I was proud of, but she was one of them.

I aimed a finger towards the bedroom area. "Bathroom's that way if you'd like to get the road dust off and clean up."

After she disappeared into the back, the sound of her rummaging through the drawers for something to put on registered. The spray of the shower sounded, and I finally closed my eyes and inhaled. I needed sleep. I needed to track down a traitorous killer within our family. I needed to find out if the hit out on me was still in effect and if it had been initiated by the same traitorous DeLuca that had set up Don Ermanno's assassination.

I couldn't recall when I had lumbered over to the couch, but I eased my head back, letting it fall into the comfort of the cushions. My gaze met the ceiling and remained there while all the details of the last few days raced through my brain, demanding attention.

"Primo," a gentle voice called. "Primo," sounded once more, ripping me away from the dream that vanished the moment I comprehended my transition from sleep to wakefulness.

There was no way not to smile when something so beautiful was filling my view. Nevah had taken her hair down, and the thick, dark tresses fell past her shoulders and fanned around her face. The warm sweet scent of whatever soap was in the bathroom commingled with her natural honey-ginger scent and had my mouth watering.

I lost the fight with my eyes, and they fell below her neck. Her tight nipples pushed against my white T-shirt she wore, the sight making me swallow to contain the sudden rush of lust that hit me.

The shirt was long enough on her that the tail teased her tempting thighs. A small strip of black peeked from under the shirt when she moved, indicating she'd fashioned a way to secure a pair of my silk boxers.

"The bathroom's free if you're ready to shower," she said, giving me a knowing smirk for the way I was undressing her with my eyes and unable to stop my tongue from sliding across my lips.

"Thank you," I finally replied, sitting up and unable to take my eyes off her even when she turned and headed back towards the bedroom. My T-shirt on her swayed to her rhythm and rose high enough to flash me peeks at her delicious brown thighs.

After a quick shower, I stepped back into the bedroom and found her lying in bed, staring absently at the ceiling. Although it was only eight p.m., she'd climbed into bed. I smiled at the sight of my side of the bed turned back. The gesture was simple but sweet and inviting. She must have understood my need for sleep, or I looked as tired as my drooping body suggested.

"What's on your mind?" I questioned. Her unblinking gaze remained pinned on the ceiling.

The act of climbing into bed with her was natural, like I'd done it a thousand times. She gave a quick smile and didn't protest my closeness, which should have been an intrusive act considering we'd just met. I lay back, comfortable on my back with my right arm tucked under my head. She sat up on her elbow facing me.

"I was allowing all that happened in the last few days to sink in. I'm trying to wrap my head around everything, but I can't help asking, *"What now?* What should I do?

How do I maneuver under these circumstances to live and find happiness?"

"There will be storms to weather, trouble that lies in wait, and danger that lurks and pops out of the darkness, but through it all, the good far outweighs the bad. A vow I made to myself on your behalf is to make sure you live well, are taken care of however you need, and to find and bring you happiness when I'm able. I intend to keep that vow, even when troubles come knocking."

The smile on her face dragged mine to the surface. I didn't know I could be that damned sappy and real with someone, but I meant every word.

"Primo?"

"Yes?"

"There is something you can do right now that would make me happy," she said. Our gazes locked so tightly, neither of us blinked. "I have no doubt that things can be good, but tomorrow is not promised. Make love to me, Primo. Fuck me. Sex me up. Screw me. It doesn't matter. I need something good right here and now."

My dick stiffened to an aching peak, so fast, it looked like it had come alive in my shorts. I sucked in a calming breath through my teeth to allow me to regain control. It didn't take me but a hot second to toss back the covers and fill my hands with those silky hips of hers.

The sight of us together was doing a number on my plans to take it slowly for our first time. Her brown and my tan skin happily mingled and created a sensory fix. The visual stimulation we created was a first, making us the living definition of an erotic episode potent enough to stimulate my senses to new heights.

My hands wouldn't stop roaming along her warm curves and the silky, glowing skin she possessed. Her body moved in sensual waves under my touch, but it wasn't enough. I needed a lot more. I needed to see if her lips were as soft as I remembered from the short kiss we shared last night.

When my lips caressed the satiny skin of her neck, her breaths blew out harder, and her hands worked my T-shirt up my sides, exposing more flesh. Her fingertips, brushing over my skin, had me releasing strangled groans. I'd never wanted every part of someone this way.

Nevah had it all, everything I wanted from the moment I laid eyes on her. The timing was fucked up, but there was nothing or no one in this world who could tell me she wasn't my woman. I knew it now. I knew it yesterday, and I'd know it years from now, even if she hadn't acknowledged it yet.

The moment her warm hands brushed my abs I was done with the foreplay dance we were doing. To establish a more secure position, I scooted back until my back rested against the cold, wooden headboard.

I lifted her fast and smoothly, making her gasp, but she caught on, dragging her legs across mine. She didn't miss a beat in our connecting rhythm, throwing her arms around my neck to add pressure to our kiss that followed.

She released a girlish giggle when I squeezed the globes of her ass and drew her in so our bodies were chest to chest. A tender kiss followed, one much too delicate for the kinds of hot shit swimming around in my head.

I obliged her with a passion that help create the energy exchange between us, the currents shooting down my body with enough force to make my toes tingle. This was new, me brimming with a rush I didn't know how to process.

Nevah eased back, flashing me heavy, seductive eyes that matched the currents flowing between us. I was a novice who didn't know shit about romance, but instincts and her responses were all the guidance I needed. My dick jerked, shifting my focus. I flashed her a touch of the raw heat rolling through me.

"You can sit there with your pussy shoved against my dick and pretend to be modest, or you can help yourself to whatever the fuck you like. Trust me, you don't want me up there until I calm down."

The comment made her lift a brow. Her tongue, wet and eager, brushed across her lips and came to rest with the tip sitting in the center of her lush top lip. I assumed she would be standoffish considering our situation, but she, like me, was unwilling to waste the opportunity. Our mutual attraction made it easy for us to demonstrate the passion we created within each other.

She reached down, sliding her hand into the top of my boxers, teasing me. She moved her fingers along the edge of the material, the back of her hand skimming my side and stomach while her eyes were fucking the shit out of me.

She glanced down, setting her eyes on the bulge waiting there for her. My erection was stretched so tight, I was sure it was strong enough to leave a bruise under her thighs. The smirk on her face was laced with a hint of something I couldn't decode. She didn't take my boxers down right away. Instead, she allowed her hands to continue to roam.

"Slide down a little," she ordered. I complied, easing down until my head rested against the pillows. My arms lay bent and tucked behind my head, waiting to witness her experience whatever her heart desired.

Her silky thighs slid along mine, spreading the warm heat between her legs on her way down. Her smile revealed the level of joy wrapped around her senses, and the emotions she experienced were playing out on her body's every erotic move.

She proceeded with a mix of tender and firm strokes, caressing my abs, and running a firm hand up and along my sides before she leaned in and placed kisses on my chest, flicking her hot tongue across my nipple. The slide of her tongue electrified my pulse and caused my blood to push through my veins like crimson heat.

I was being seduced, another new experience, but one that was so hot and sexy, I fed on the heady vibes. Nevah was taking inventory, inspecting, and marking her territory. Her exploring hands were in sync with the flow of her entrancing body.

"You like what you see, *il mio cuore batte?*"

She nodded, and although she couldn't translate me calling her *my heartbeat*, the knowing in her gaze said that she understood that a deeper meaning was being expressed.

Her hand slipped around my hard dick through the hole of my boxers and gave it a gentle squeeze. Lust grew heavy in her eyes at the enticing touch and my groaning reaction.

"I like what I feel too," she said before removing her hand and tugging at the sides of my boxers to take them down. I didn't waste any time helping her to help me out of them.

"Mmm," she moaned, her eyes on my dick standing in a full and proud salute. She cupped it securely in her palms before sliding her hands up and down with a delicate stroke that closed my eyes.

My eyes popped back open when she repositioned herself between my legs and handled my dick like she knew it belonged to her. A hot shot of lust raced through me when her sweet lips touched down and placed a gentle kiss on the tip of my leaking head.

Fuck, she's killing me.

Her tempting mouth remained in place, letting my dick push her lips apart until they were wrapped around the head. Her movements were deliberate, hot. She turned me on so fiercely, I fought to keep from coming with the first dip her mouth took down my length.

Shit.

My fist clenched tight, and a low growl teased the back of my throat at the sight of her making me disappear into her mouth until the head pressed the back of her throat. Those seductive eyes glanced up and met mine, making me want more while luring me deeper into our connection.

She enjoyed this, and judging by the smile in her gaze, she wanted my eyes on her. One of her attentive hands held my dick steady while her pleasing mouth gave it a warm, wet massage. Her lips, her tongue, even the delicate graze of her teeth drove uncut pleasure into me, making me thrust against her face.

Her other hand explored my chest, abs, and thighs, dipping into grooves, pinching skin hard and soft, and rubbing firm and light. She didn't waste a touch, a kiss, or a lick. She used every moving part to make me appreciate the sensations coursing through me.

"Fuck, that feels good," I whispered, enjoying the way she was pleasing me.

When she used her hands and gave my dick maximum attention by taking it deeply into her mouth, working her tongue along the bottom of my tightly stretched shaft, my damn toes curled tight enough to make my bones crack.

"Fuck. Don't stop. Take it all in. Shit. Yes!"

The explosion of pleasure hit so hard that I jerked up off the bed before I fell into a blissfully orgasmic state of mind, strong enough to make my heart jump in my chest. When my head stopped floating, all I could do was lie there and blink. I didn't feel bad about coming so damn fast because my dick was already reclaiming its hard, authoritative stance.

A newfound energy kicked in and I sat up in a rush, helping her out of her shirt and licking my lips at the sight of her sizable round tits. My eager hand stroked down the center of her chest until I was at my boxers that she wore. A hard yank and pull had me zipping them down her legs and off of her so swiftly, she glanced down and back up at me with a big *O* of surprise on her face.

"Center of the bed. On your back. Now!" I growled, loving how her eyes lit up at my demand. She moved swiftly, scooting up and shifting her body into position.

"Open those sexy legs. Let me see."

Her legs fell apart with ease, her flower parting like a curtain opening to reveal the grand prize. Her lips were plump and beautiful, the perfect petals that encircled her bud. The sight of it peeking out had my mouth watering and me swallowing back the explosion of lust threatening to consume me.

Her hand ran along her squirming body, her fingers fondling her perky left tit and squeezing her taut, dark brown nipple before she lowered her dancing fingers across her stomach.

"Stop," I called out.

Her middle finger was extended and sat at the apex of her sex. She wasn't cognizant of what she was about to do, but it pleased me to see that she wasn't afraid to touch herself.

"This is my pussy now," I told her, sending a roving eye along her naked body. "You have to ask me for permission to *touch* from now on."

I climbed over one of her splayed legs while her head shook in a quick and obedient nod.

"Lie back and relax while I show you how good I treat *my* pussy."

My heavy but slow hands slid under the backs of her thighs, lifting her legs higher and spreading her open further. Her nectar seeped, coating her lips and making her pearl sparkle. The sight and the scent she produced formed a mix that enticed me to lick my lips while my nostrils flared. Never in my life had a woman smelled so damn good and had a pussy so visually mouthwatering, I salivated for a taste.

I was unaware that I was lowering my mouth to her pussy the entire time until the shadow of her open legs cast against my vision. My tongue met her lips, which were warm and succulent and the first hit of her flavor on my tongue was a divine intoxication. I couldn't get enough of her, lapping up her juices with well-placed licks and sucking kisses.

While my mouth and tongue worked, I memorized her every tantalizing response. The pleasing way her moans teased my eardrums. The way her inner thighs worked to thrust her soaked pussy at my face. The way she teased, pinched, and twisted one of her nipples between her fingers while she fisted the covers with her other hand. The way her sparkling-sweet taste lit up my taste buds and caused me to lick faster and harder to savor every last drop of her flavor. The sight of our entrancing swirl...

Damn!

Her moans grew more intense and her breathing erratic, every breath chased by a throaty moan of pleasure. She came fast, hard and screaming my name, her pussy quivering against my tongue and her body dancing in uncontrolled delight.

"Oh. Primo! Yes, Primo, yes!"

After I tongue-stroked her with light flicks back to reality, I glanced up to find her covering her face with one hand.

"Sorry, it's been a while."

"You have nothing to be sorry about because we are going to see about keeping you on a steady regimen of orgasms until one or both of our bodies decides to stop working."

Her eyes went wide, but it wasn't fear flashing in her glazed-over glint. She nodded, flashing me a cute smirk that enticed my grin to surface.

Chapter Sixteen

Nevah

The tremble in my thighs continued. My still uneven breaths caught when Primo ran his big strong hands up my legs. The desire he stirred refused to be stifled by my physical limitations. I hadn't had sex in so long that I couldn't recall if it was seven, eight, or maybe even nine months since my pussy had been in use.

The act of doing it myself was so mundane and boring that I would roll onto my stomach, finger myself until I conjured up a mediocre orgasm, and fall asleep.

Primo licked my aching nipples before circling one and sucking it into his mouth with a delicious pressure that had me swiveling my hips to calm the throbbing need terrorizing my core. He switched, sucking the other, the action drawing a strangled moan from my throat and sending a pang of fiery lust to my core. A warm gush of wetness seeped out in a steady hot flow and drizzled down my inner thigh.

"Oh!" I cried out when his quick hand slid between my legs, and two thick and long fingers brushed past the slick heat of my wet lips and glided into my starved pussy. My nipple being licked and tugged between his teeth and his fingers sliding in and out of me was so deliciously arousing that my quick-coming ass would burst again if he kept this type of play going.

"Feels like you're ready for me," he said.

My head probably resembled a bobblehead, I shook it so fast. My tongue clicked on the roof of my mouth, nipples tingling and pussy hot and aching. I was filled with an eagerness I'd never experienced. Primo's movements threw me off until I noticed the condom in his hand after he made it appear out of thin air, a part of the magic act he was performing on me so far.

Blessedly, he kept those gift-giving fingers of his shoved deep inside me while he turned slightly, ripping through the condom with his teeth. His multitasking game was on point as I squirmed against his fingers while watching him spit a piece of the condom wrapper off his lips in the process of slipping it along his impressive length.

He lifted up, his eyes on mine before he extracted his fingers and eased into position, preparing to calm the ache screaming its demands for the thick treat my eyes were feasting on. The head, so warm and hard, sat at my wet lips, slicing across them before they opened to the pressure he applied. My eyes fell closed, afraid that if I saw him enter me, I'd come on impact.

"Eyes open," he growled while he sank the first few inches deeper, taking the little bit of air I managed to pull into my lungs. It was difficult keeping my eyes open through the process of him stretching me to fit him. Prickles of pleasure zipped up my spine, making my inner thighs quiver as I focused on his penetrating gaze.

"Mmm." The moaning tickled my throat, the sound producing a low level of pleasure. My teeth bit deep into my lip before my nails sank deeper into his hard bicep and rippling side. He eased back and pushed in until he drove every inch into me, filling me up to the point that pain and pleasure formed a pact to give the most entrancing sexual stimulation imaginable.

Instead of a moan, the word, "Shit!" was mixed with the deep breath that was forced out of my lungs and past my quivering lips.

"Fuck," Primo gritted out low in my ear, unable to keep the slow, deliberate, and demanding thrusts that were the equivalent to perfection. The tremble in his body gave a hint at the amount of effort he was pouring into making this a mutually beneficial exchange for us.

He stilled while my pussy clenched uncontrollably around him, adjusting, applauding, cheering, and grateful to have company this good inside her. The resistance my walls were inflicting on his dick was revealing the long stretch of time that I'd been without.

"Mmm!" My noisy moan was enough to ward off the overwhelming ache of another orgasm making an attempt to take me out already. Primo slowed his stroke and distracted me with a soul-stirring kiss that brought me back from the brink of letting the pleasure control my mind.

We picked up a rhythm together, my pussy gripping and slurping to counter the aggressive beatdown he was delivering. It was the kind of pounding that reverberated in my stomach and that I knew would leave me aching so good, I'd turn private investigator and stake out places in search of the dick.

Our bodies kissed, my hard nipples rubbing the short hairs on his chest, while I soaked up the aching stimulation that shot heat to my core. His lips, warm and smooth, brushed pure heat against my neck while I used his pec for a muzzle.

My teeth sank deep into his deliciously taut flesh. My licks and sucks fell in time with the pounding strokes, each delivering the maximum desired effect of pleasure, kissed by delicious pain.

"Pree-mo!" I moaned, the only way I knew to express the impact each deep, downward grind delivered. When he increased the pace, the hard thrust filled me up one moment while dragging out pleasure the next.

Wild was too tame a word for my gripping, tugging, yelling, and pelvic thrusting reactions. I held on tight, squeezing him against me like I was trying to make my body devour his whole.

"Oh! There. There. There," I yelled like a madwoman when he hit a spot I was sure had never been stroked. A fire within a fire was lit, and compounding pleasure built into something that threatened to rip me apart.

"Right here?" he asked before plunging deep and hitting the spot over and over until my body dissolved, and I turned into a bed of straight *fuck-me-until-I-come!*

"Yes. Yes. Fuck me!" I yelled out with a shrieking cry mixed with a moan and didn't stop until the need for air prompted me to inhale.

A strong arm was wedged under my thigh, lifting and hooking my leg in place. The repositioning sent him so deep into my pulsating heat, I found a way to grip his flexing ass and rode the thick wave of pleasure until I screamed down the walls.

"Oh. Oh, God!" I was done, coming so good, and long, and hard, I think the extreme bliss temporarily shattered my mind. Tiny prickles of darkness evaded the bright brilliance that filled me to the brink of breaking me before it exploded, and wave after wave of pulsing pleasure peeled back in layers until I was as light as a feather.

Primo chased the high I was experiencing, fucking me so hard and untamed my body tensed and released while my pussy endured the most severely delicious beating of her life. The sounds we created were full-bodied and delivered enough force that it snatched my dwindling desire and spiked the ache back to an insatiable need.

Another orgasm roared to life inside me, and the burst of sharp tingles fell in sync with Primo's so that we enjoyed the rush together.

The afterglow left me smiling stupidly at the ceiling, while continuing to twitch with delight and tingle with sensual joy.

Chapter Seventeen

Primo

My fingers traced along Nevah's damp shoulder before I leaned in and placed a kiss there. We had gone at it three times, and I hadn't had enough and wasn't sure if I ever would get enough of her. My usual sexual encounters, if you could call them that, were fuck, make the woman come a time or two, get mine, and move on. Half the time, we didn't even bother exchanging names.

What was so different about Nevah that she could make me want her like this? What did she possess that made me want to find a place for her in my life when my life was literally organized chaos?

Grade A addictive pussy for starters. A physical and mental connection that I still need time to figure out. Smart. Career minded. A shapely body type that has my name stamped on it. And a pretty face to top it all off.

What was there not to like? I couldn't have built a more perfect woman for myself if I had the app to do so. From where I was sitting, I considered myself one lucky motherfucker.

Nope.

I shook my head when the disturbing thought of letting her go surfaced.

Nevah fell under what I was appropriately calling the learn-as-you-go relationship program. I didn't give a damn if she turned out to be the most annoying person on the planet; I couldn't picture me without her now that we were together.

"So the old Don, Don Ermanno, was assassinated, and Don Enzo is now running the family."

It was a statement. She was soaking up the DeLuca family history and knowledge I was giving her while remaining an active participant in the best and only sex marathon I'd had the pleasure of experiencing. Her interest was all the proof I needed to know that she no longer held on to the illusion of a life of white picket fences.

***

Hours later.

We had gotten a decent amount of sleep, considering we'd squeezed in a fourth round of sex and another hour of insightful conversation that gave me a snapshot of her life. Although her father had stepped out on her drug addicted mother when she was a baby, Nevah had been smart and strong enough to overcome her neighborhood, abuse at her mother's hand, and attend and do impressively well in college.

We eased out of bed at eight, the latest I'd slept in twenty years, showered together, and dressed.

She was the first woman who'd cooked for me, another remarkable quality to add to the collection of reasons I wasn't letting her go.

She happily served me a veggie omelet, toast, and orange juice. Her company was so enjoyable we didn't walk out the door until ten a.m. It was time she received a glimpse into a few of my daily duties.

Nevah reminded me that she planned on being at my side no matter the situation. She had nailed home the point last night while riding my dick like she'd bought and purchased it.

As much as I was against her becoming that up close to my work life, she hadn't given me the option of saying no. At that moment, balls deep inside her with her twirling on my dick, I would have told her whatever she wanted to hear. The moment things settled into a sense of normality in our family, she'd understand that being my shadow wasn't necessary.

My gaze landed on my driver's side mirror. Could the black Lincoln MKZ I spotted two miles and four turns back be officially labeled a tail?

The Vittorio family should have called off any more threats they had out on me if they possessed any self-preservation instincts and wanted to prevent war. The DeLuca who was working with them might as well put a gun in their mouth and pull the trigger. They were free, for now, but I'd caught their scent and wasn't going to stop until their soul was breaking out of their body to find a safer place than in the same space as me.

Repressing a sigh of frustration, I ran several different scenarios through my head on how this was all going to go down, and none of them involved me dying. A few car rides as my new shadow, and Nevah was about to get her second taste of what it meant to be a DeLuca.

"If I asked you to marry me right now, would you?" I blurted the question, not sure where the hell it had come from all of a sudden.

Her lips fell apart, and her unblinking gaze met mine and froze. I could almost picture the different scenarios running through her head based on what I knew was a difficult question to answer.

Her chin dipped at her hard swallow. "If you asked me to marry you…" Her head dipped, her eyes dropping to her hands sitting in her lap. She lifted her gaze to meet mine, hers shining with a bright sparkle I'd never seen in them before. "If you asked, I'd say yes."

My big grin must have enticed hers because we basked in the moment before I leaned in, and she met me halfway for a quick emotion-laced kiss. Who the hell was I with this woman?

"So, fiancée, I'm about to make you another promise."

A slow smile creased her sexy lips, and concern seeped into her expression when I didn't return one.

"I'll fight for you until my last breath and will give my life to save yours. I'd vow not to put you in harm's way, but you kind of took that option away when you insisted on being my shadow." I glanced in the mirror and spotted the trailing car. "The DeLuca name comes with a lot of danger attached to it. Are you up for that kind of excitement?"

"Oddly, with you, I can't imagine anything else. But, to answer your question, I believe I'm ready."

Another glance in the mirror confirmed that there wasn't one vehicle trailing us, but two. The second vehicle was a dark gray BMW.

"That being said, I need you to get down," I told her before reaching over, moving her seatbelt strap from over her shoulder, and pulling her down until the side of her head was resting against my thigh.

"Primo, what's about to happen?" she questioned, her voice strained with tension.

"We have two tails. I believe it's members of the same crew that came after me the night we met."

I stroked her lovely face with the back of my fingers, her wide, frightened eyes holding mine. "Whatever you do, don't get up unless I say it's okay."

Her shaky, "Okay," sounded. Her breaths rushed out while one of her hands clung to my shirt at my lower back and her other to a chunk of my thigh.

"When I said I'd protect you with my life, you believed me, right?"

"Yes. I believe you." The confirmation reflected in her eyes reinforced her words.

All the windows came down, the wind hitting me in the face like a teasing slap. A glimpse of my reflection in the rearview mirror revealed my tight-face and stress level, not for my own well-being but for Nevah's. I hated that she was involved in this part of the deadly business I usually handled alone. The idea of her enduring even a second of it tugged at my heart, ripping pieces away.

However, I'd been trained to be tough, unbending, and savage blood pumped through my veins. There was more than family in my life to fight for now, and I'd fuck up the devil and run hell before I let anyone take Nevah away from me.

The pursuing vehicles were closing in on us, and The Mustang GT500 we had stopped and traded the Nissan for answered my demanding request for speed, the engine roaring with strength and readiness. The BMW took a few major roadway risks to catch me, growling with its bumper gearing up to ram mine.

The force of the momentum when they hit connected with my bumper on the second attempt, sending our bodies lurching forward before the screeching tires sounded. My seatbelt and the one around Nevah's lower body kept me from smashing into the steering wheel and her into the dash display. The tight straps yanked hard enough to hurt. My arms worked against opposing forces, twisting and turning to keep us from crashing into other unsuspecting drivers.

The BMW that rammed us had done it at the detriment of their own vehicle, not considering that they would give me the upper hand they assumed would be in their favor. I'd wanted them to hit us so that I could turn the steering wheel just before they struck again.

My defensive driving took us out of their path and led to them having to slam on the brakes. Their tires screamed and spat out smoke from the burning rubber to avoid a high-speed crash with an RV.

Once they straightened, they geared up again and successfully rammed us this time. The hard bump turned out to be the exact boost we needed. We swerved into the lane to my left that was thankfully clear. The tires released a boisterously long screech, protesting my sudden braking.

The momentum of the turn had us at its mercy inside the vehicle. My arms burned with the effort it was taking to get us aligned in a position of opportunity, which was facing our attackers.

We turned at least a half-circle before the vehicle came to a stop on the edge of the median. My silenced pistol was out the window, and two slugs were released as quickly and as rapidly as my heartbeats. Death was on a mission, moving towards the BMW driver's head.

The man was so focused on controlling his vehicle that he was too late to react to what was already in play. The impact of the first bullet when it struck him in the head released a spray of blood so visually dramatic, it didn't even appear real. The second bullet landed in his chest, the force of the impact shoving his body into the seat. He jerked, disrupting his motor functions enough to start the car's rapid acceleration.

His slumped body continued to steer the car, his hand likely death-gripped around the steering wheel, and his leg locked in place on the accelerator. The car rolled past us and its trajectory had it heading for the concrete barrier about three car lengths ahead.

The Lincoln was making its rapid approach. The dark shadows of the driver and passenger became more pronounced by the time I got us moving again.

The target's body in the runaway and now crashed BMW had somehow found a way to lay on the horn, his last act before dying. The horn bellowed a continuous death shriek into the sky. Nevah squeezed me to her like her life depended on it, her eyes shut so tightly I could see them trembling even in the midst of battle.

My foot stomped on the gas hard and fast, gunning the engine, my actions lifting Nevah about as high as my chest. We shot off like a bat in danger of catching a fire-ball to the ass thrown from the devil's hands.

The Lincoln gave chase, zooming around cars to keep up with my own evasive maneuvering.

Thump! Thump! Thump!

The bullets struck but didn't penetrate the hull of my car. Since there were two individuals in the pursuing vehicle, one had the advantage of shooting while the other drove.

"Nevah, I need a favor."

"Yes." The word sounded just above a whisper.

"Stay down, but I need you to reach up and grab my phone. Your thumbprint will unlock it. Dial Franco, number six on the list."

I sensed her eyeing me when she used her thumbprint to get into my phone, but she didn't comment. She would learn that I didn't snooze on *anything* because being lazy in this family and in my line of work was a hazard to one's health.

"Primo?"

Thankfully, Franco answered after my *fiancée* did what I'd asked of her before placing her head back against my thigh.

"Are you at work?"

"Yes," he answered.

Franco was one of the best sharpshooters I knew. He had spent ten years in the military before a roadside bomb in Iraq took one of his legs. He wasn't a DeLuca by blood, but he had become family years ago.

"I'll be there in about seven minutes. I have a tail I need you to cut off."

"Okay, I'll be ready," he said before clicking off. More shots struck the vehicle, one breaking the driver's side mirror but left the housing in place. They did the same to the passenger side, attempting to blind me. However, I didn't need mirrors for where I was heading.

I glanced down at the beautiful woman clinging to me, and even while bullets were flying, having her fill my vision brought a smile to my face. The quick jerk I gave the steering wheel kept the asshole from rear-ending us. I turned into the swerve before jerking hard in the opposite direction to prevent a head-on collision with an oncoming SUV.

The Lincoln was nearly clipped on the driver's side but avoided the accident to maintain the chase. I saw the parking lot of the aluminum recycling warehouse I needed to enter about a quarter of a mile away. Franco had opened the gates, and all I needed to do was decelerate enough to make the sharp turn.

I swerved into the turn at forty-five mph, the vehicle screeching and leaning hard enough to send Nevah sliding towards the passenger door, but she held strong.

The Lincoln was right on my tail, the vehicle screeching its way into the lot after us. As soon as I was at least two car lengths ahead and roaring across the lot like a runaway train, multiple rounds of gunfire pelted the Lincoln, lighting it up like fireworks in celebration of our victory.

"God," Nevah called out as her fingers managed to dig deeper into my leg.

I came to a screeching stop, the Mustang rocking harshly before I cut the engine.

"No matter what you hear, I need you to stay inside this vehicle."

"Okay," she said, unbuckling and sliding to the passenger side floor. Her wide gaze met mine and held before I lifted my pistol, flung my door open, and hopped out.

The Lincoln had come to a dead sideways stop, tires shot out, engine blown, and the passenger's head blown off, with most of it likely spread across the back seat. Smoke billowed thick and black from the front of the car. A few quick steps closer to the driver's side showed him attempting to free himself from the seat belt.

His head jerked frantically around while lifting and taking quick peeks over the steering wheel and ducking as quickly. He had no idea who was shooting at him or which direction the next shot would be fired from. The passenger's head resembling a dropped pot of beef stew added to the driver's current state of alarm.

He gave up his attempts to undo the seatbelt and lifted his pistol. The sight of me shaking my head in warning stopped him from making the deadly mistake. The gun dropped when he opened his palm and lifted his hands in surrender.

I drew closer, using a tactical approach with my pistol drawn, in case he decided he wanted to pick up his weapon and get what was coming to him.

At the driver's side window, I turned my non-gun hand in a circle, indicating that he could roll down his window, the only part of the car that wasn't decorated with bullet holes. The man shuddered like it wasn't ninety plus degrees outside, and fear seeped from his pores like sweat.

"Tell me who sent you, and I'll make your death a quick and painless one," I offered.

His body rocked back and forth, his way of dealing with the horror awaiting him. He cast a quick glance at his headless friend whose brain matter had splashed across the right side of his face.

"I don't know who it was," he forced out the shaky words. "All I was told was that it was a DeLuca. We were contacted, hired, and sent to an abandoned warehouse for the first half of the payment. The man there never revealed himself. I was just doing what I was hired to do."

"That's what they all say right before I do what comes naturally and extricate their souls from their bodies. Get the fuck out!"

He flashed a confused look like he didn't understand my words. The door creaked open from his slow movement. His bugged-out eyes remained pinned on me. I waved him over using the gun.

"Take me to the warehouse, and I'll let you walk."

He snickered sarcastically. "You expect me to believe that shit? You're a DeLuca."

He was right in his assessment because the only place I intended for him to walk was into a graveyard to pick out his plot.

"I don't expect you to do anything but climb out of that car and show me where that fucking warehouse is located."

He sat in silent contemplation before shoving the door open further. I shoved my pistol down the back of my pants and received an *are-you-crazy* side-eye before his eyes dropped to my empty hands. My ego was big, but not stupid. One of the best snipers I knew was watching my ass, and I knew more than twenty ways to kill this man with my bare hands.

He stepped out and walked ahead of me towards my vehicle.

"Stop," I called out when he was near the trunk. I reached under the latch and disengaged it before pointing inside.

"Use those to clean yourself up. I have precious cargo in the cab and can't have you contaminating the air."

He wiped the blood and brain matter from his face before I rearranged our seating, placing Nevah in the back passenger seat and him up front.

Before driving off, I gave Franco a final salute of thanks and turned back the way I'd entered, leaving the carnage for him to clean up.

Chapter Eighteen

Primo

The ride was a long maze of highways, streets, and road-ways that led us to two wrong locations before we were finally driving past the place where he claimed he'd picked up the first half of his payment.

When I drove up to the warehouse and around the side, the man's wide eyes bounced back and forth between me and the front view through the windshield. I rolled up to the door and waved at the camera he couldn't see before the wide double doors opened, and I drove inside. The men inside the warehouse were hard at work as usual and some waved upon seeing me.

"Get out," I called to my passenger, who sat slack jawed and gawking around the warehouse. A forklift was in the distance, lifting and stacking large crates, and a few men used pallet jacks to move boxes and stack others. I glanced back at an observing Nevah, who exited the back of the car on the driver's side. Her questioning gaze met mine.

"Stay close to my side."

She nodded before taking the few steps that had her shoulder brushing my arm. Cautious steps inched my guest forward before I pointed him in the direction I wanted him to walk.

"Primo!" Big Bear, another one of my many cousins, called out. It was his way of greeting me.

"How's it going?"

"All good," he replied, lifting a large box that should have been moved by a forklift and proving why he was called Big Bear instead of his given name, Tomme. His eyes were on my current company. He inched his head up at the man, asking who it was without saying a word.

I lifted a hand, letting him know not to worry about it. He cast a glance and attempted but failed to hide the smile he flashed in Nevah's direction before returning his attention back to his work.

Eyes came at us from every direction as we walked. I hadn't introduced the man on purpose, checking to see if anyone would react with suspicion about seeing him. They were all well informed about me having a woman in my life and appeared more concerned at getting a good look at Nevah than they were about the stranger I'd brought into our warehouse.

Since she'd washed and put on the same outfit from the club, I figured it would be difficult for some of the men to resist staring at the way those jeans hugged her teasing curves or the way the heels extended her long legs. Maybe it was just too hard to ignore the pretty face complementing her body.

"Primo. Didn't expect to see you today. Who's that?" Brizio asked when we walked into the office he was temporarily occupying. He bore the same curious glint about the man as the rest of the guys.

"Have a seat," I commanded my guest, pointing him to a ratty leather couch sitting against the wall facing the desk Brizio sat behind. I positioned myself on the side of the desk to have the best view of the man and be able to talk to my cousin.

Nevah was at my side, her small hand clamped around my forearm. Brizio was in the room the night Nevah and I had met, but I hadn't officially introduced them to each other.

"Brizio, this is Nevah. Nevah, my cousin Brizio," I introduced her.

Brizio's gaze flashed recognition and his wide smile greeted her before he reached out and took her free hand.

"Good to see you again."

"You too," she said.

He held her hand long enough for me to flash him a death stare. When I reached up, palmed his grinning face, and shoved him away from her, he released a loud outburst of laughter.

"Never thought I'd see the fucking day that *it* actually happened to Hades himself," he said, his teasing laughter ongoing.

Nevah's forehead pinched at his reaction, unaware that her being at my side in any room was about as rare as a bigfoot sighting.

"Nevah. I'm the cousin you can call when this dry-as-toast ogre bores you to death."

His comment won him a heart-warming smile before she mouthed, "Okay."

Once he'd shown Nevah that he could be fun-loving and friendly, Brizio's cold gaze landed on the man sitting on the couch, who met that gaze with an expression that suggested he wanted to throw up.

"Who do we have here?" Brizio questioned, his gaze zeroing in on the man like he'd locked on to a target he was preparing to destroy.

"He and his buddies just tried to kill me. Had to get Franco involved. This one said he came to this location to pick up the first payment for the hit that was put out on me."

"What the fuck? You don't believe that shit, do you?" Brizio questioned, his face tight with disbelief. "I believe I'd know if there was a fucking diseased rat among the crew. I'll vouch for every man out there."

"I believe you, cousin. I marched him past the crew without saying who he was, and their reactions were similar to yours."

"Did you see the man who paid you the money?" Brizio questioned the man. He shook his head while his gaze bounced back and forth between Brizio and me.

"You mind keeping Nevah company while I conduct a more thorough walkthrough with him? I need to find out something today before I make another decision I can't take back."

Brizio nodded, his cold gaze raking over the man before he glanced at Nevah and allowed his smile to return. On my way out, Brizio asked Nevah, "How's that messy friend of yours, Maya is it?"

So that's where the recognition came from between Brizio and Nevah. He and I were going to have to have a talk. Him getting involved with anyone Nevah knew was out of the question. I didn't need him messing up shit in my relationship when he pissed her friend off with his craziness. The fact that he was even asking about her already spelled trouble.

***

Half an hour of show-and-tell hadn't gotten me any definitive answers. The men didn't know this man, and he didn't recognize any of them.

"Take me to the spot where you received your payment."

He nodded, his head moving robotically with hope flashing in his wide eyes. "The building was empty except for the person I was supposed to meet. I was on the phone with him while he directed me into the building and to that spot," he said, pointing at our interrogation area which was actually two connecting offices set up with a two-way mirror between them.

"The door to that office was closed, so I was directed into that one. I never saw the person I was talking to, although I sensed them watching me. The envelope of cash was sitting on the desk like they had stated."

I didn't react, although I wanted to choke the life from him for taking a payment to take my life.

"So you never heard the person's voice other than on the phone? Did you see the person's face?"

He shook his head, confirming my questions. The person he met could have been anyone.

Who the fuck had access to our warehouse and had the balls to bring in and pay off the person they were hiring to kill me?

"They did have a distinct scent," he added, his wide, hopeful gaze pinned on my face like his information would somehow keep him away from his date with death. "It was like spicy black licorice."

A long silent stare was what I offered the man after his admission, as ideas on who wanted me dead churned in my head. When I finally decided to move, I led him to the most open part of the warehouse floor after texting Brizio to leave Nevah in the office and meet me.

The man and I stood in the center of the warehouse like we were buddies. I had no doubt that he had an idea of what was coming. I allowed hundreds of scenarios to run rampant through my head on who the bold DeLuca motherfucker was who was still aiming to kill me after we had destroyed their connection with the Vittorio family.

Brizio walked up and stood on the other side of the man, whose watery eyes and tension-filled body was overdosing on fear. I quoted Brizio a quick rundown on what I discovered about the payment and how it was delivered.

"Can I have your attention, please?" Brizio called out, his voice carrying in the open space easily. Movement stopped, pallet jacks stopped rolling, and soon after, the aggressive roar of the forklift's engine died.

The men gathered around us, some emerging from dark corners and hidden areas. When at least twenty surrounded us, I observed their behavior with keen interest. There was no doubt that a DeLuca had paid men to kill me, but I no longer believed it was any of the men in this building.

"This man," Brizio aimed a thumb at the man whose head dropped while his lips moved in prayer, "and two of his friends just tried to assassinate our Capo." Brizio's announcement drew a round of protest and curses from the group. "The rest of his friends who went after Primo are dead, but this one claims to have been paid money inside this warehouse by a DeLuca to complete the job."

The news got the men riled up. I lifted my hands and lowered them with ease to calm them.

"I know that it was none of you who betrayed the DeLuca name, but I need you all to keep an eye out for any DeLuca rat that has been or may act suspicious. Don't alert them that you're on to them but inform Brizio or me of what you see."

A round of agreeing voices sounded before hushed whispers swirled around the crowd.

"I need you to show this motherfucker what happens when they try to kill me and don't succeed."

Pipes, sticks, metal posts, and anything that could inflict pain were sought out and picked up. There were a few men pounding their fist into their palms, preparing to pound flesh. Brizio was standing there smiling like I'd announced him the winner of the lottery.

"This was one job you should have turned down," I told the man before I walked away. My men approached the trembling man, their eyes ravenous and their snarls and grumbles vicious.

When I opened the door to the office, Nevah was sitting on the couch, her lips pinched tightly between her teeth as stress lines stretched across her forehead. The brutally savage murder taking place behind me sounded before I closed the door and muffled the noise.

Nevah was up and at my side and in my arms without me having to say a word. Our pull towards each other, although alarmingly compulsive, was something I hoped would never dull.

"Are you okay? Did you find out who's trying to kill you?"

"No, but I think I'm getting closer to narrowing down an answer. They used this warehouse to set up another DeLuca to take the fall, unaware that I know most of these guys better than they know themselves."

I squeezed her tight against my body. Did she have any idea she was the only woman I'd ever had a desire to be this way with? All that had occurred in the past forty-eight hours had faded into the background because of her. When my heart made an attempt to escape my chest to get to her, I released her too quickly, failing to temper the emotional rush that had taken control. She flashed me a questioning glint but didn't comment.

"Let's get out of here. There's a bit of brutal business being handled, so we'll take the long way around."

Her head shook in a slow, disagreeing gesture. "Let's go the way we came. We are together now, so I need to see what I may not want to see. I need to know what I may not want to know. I need to experience what being with you is truly like in the good times, bad times, and times when business is being handled. I can't be with you and be blind or weak. It will make me easy prey, and it will make you weaker for being worried about me."

"Where have you been all my life?" I genuinely wanted to know.

Her shoulders lifted in a light shrug before I opened the door, and the sound of a dying man's cries found our ears. The wet, fleshy *thumps* matched the bloody scene. They were going to be cleaning up blood splatter for a week and sweeping up a few of his parts with a broom.

Nevah clasped a hand around mine while we walked, a foreign action I was learning to settle into because of her. My track record with women had been so uninspiring that us walking hand in hand drew attention from an active murder scene, causing necks to swivel and curious eyes to track our movements.

A quick wave came our way from Brizio before he turned back, lifted a pipe, and slammed it down on what was left of the man.

Chapter Nineteen

Primo

My way of life involved looking over my shoulder for the trouble that would assuredly chase me. However, casting that same eye for the usual chaos plus assassins hired to kill me by a member of my own fucking family was an inconvenience.

Though reluctant, I answered my phone that wouldn't stop ringing.

"Hello."

"Primo," Brizio called out. He was breathing so hard, I hardly made out that it was him.

"You better not be on this fucking phone having sex again while calling me about business," I warned him.

"No sex but the next best thing," he said with a snicker.

"You remember the two who were stupid enough to follow you into the bathroom?"

"Yes. I remember."

"The man you left with me. I damaged him too badly the first night, so he needed a little time to recover before he could speak again. Anyway, I discovered that he was tied to the ones who tried to take Leandra. They were a part of the same crew that he claimed were a seven man team. They are not connected to the crew sent by the Vittorio family so they are working off of two different contracts under two different agendas. Which means there are more hitmen out there unaccounted for. Are Lenni and Umberto still watching Leandra?"

"Yes, they still have eyes on her and *them*."

"Good," Brizio said. "The man, may he rest in pieces, couldn't tell me who hired them. The person covered their tracks well enough that the people they hired are clueless about their identity. But, I did get out of him that he believed it was a DeLuca, like we already know, and that they had strict orders to keep tabs on Leandra, I believe as a means of getting to you."

"I suspected as much. Fuck," I muttered under my breath.

"You got anything planned," Brizio asked, too enthusiastic about the prospect of shedding blood.

"No," I said, glancing over at Nevah, who was watching me like a little hawk. Based on the little furrow in her brow, she knew trouble was stirring.

"Let me know if you need me," Brizio added.

"I will. Thank you," I said before hanging up.

***

The restaurant I currently sat in was owned by my family, and although I should have been comfortable, an edgy feeling rested on my shoulders and my trigger finger was tingling. However, this was where my nose and the hard work of my people had led me in the hunt for the DeLuca rat who had a hard on for my death.

"Hi, Primo," a female voice sang.

"Hello, Leandra."

I eyed the piece of material wrapped around her breasts and ass. There wasn't much left to anyone's imagination. If you slept with Leandra, you pretty much knew most of what you were going to get beforehand.

"May I?" she said, pointing at the seat Nevah had vacated to go to the restroom.

I nodded.

"I saw you and wanted to say a quick hello. Is everything all right? I mean, I know it isn't all right with all that's been going on, but is there anything I can do to help?"

My head shook. "I'm close to solving our traitor problem, and you won't have to worry about staying low-key anymore."

Her smile came easily, and her roaming gaze raked over me in that way it always did, letting me know she hadn't lost interest.

"Is she having trouble adjusting to the DeLuca way of life?" she questioned, glancing in the direction Nevah had walked.

My shoulders lifted casually, not confirming or denying anything. I was smart enough not to reveal to a woman that was interested in me the business between me and the woman I was with. Leandra could assume whatever the hell she wanted.

"If you'd like, maybe I can speak to her, show her the ropes of how to be a loyal DeLuca woman."

"That's nice of you, but I'll handle it."

I didn't miss the sneaky smile in her gaze at my words. She didn't think me and Nevah would be together for very long.

"She's not going to last in this family," she stated casually, referring to Nevah and confirming what I'd read in her gaze. "I can tell it at a glance. She's one of those high-maintenance women that's more suited for a suit and tie, straight-laced businessman."

I didn't comment. This was the norm with Leandra and me. She talked, and most times I'd let her while her words failed to make any type of lasting impact

My fingers rubbed at my beard while I eyed her with suspicion. Her hopeful gaze begged for a chance despite Nevah being near.

Why was this woman so interested in me? I was a dick most of the time, and she knew my track record with women didn't include long-term relationships. It may have been why she was disrespecting Nevah like I'd already given her walking papers.

I believe it was time I took Leandra up on her offer to help me. I hated to go down this road with her, but she would eventually find out that I wasn't worth the trouble she poured into trying to get my attention.

"Call me later. I believe I have a job for you." I gave her a perceptive nod when I noticed Nevah exiting the restroom in the window's distorted reflection. Leandra glanced over my shoulder at Nevah before returning her attention to me.

"I'll call you later," she said, standing. The glee in her face wasn't missed. It was time I used every trick up my sleeve if I was going to flush out the DeLuca traitor among us.

When Leandra bumped into Nevah, on purpose I'm sure, I cringed.

After taking her seat, Nevah asked. "Who was that?" She flashed me a look I'd never seen in her eyes. Sharp and unblinking, it clearly said, I better not lie to her.

"Her name is Leandra DeLuca," I started and didn't end until Nevah knew Leandra's history. There was no accurate way to describe Leandra's interest in me, but I mentioned it, which only resulted in Nevah lifting a territorial brow that, of all things, turned me on.

Nevah's lack of a vocal response during this particular history lesson and her subtle expressions, facial and body language, were saying, *'bitch better back off'* and *'he is mine.'*

I had never been claimed before because I had never gone far enough with a woman to reach this point. Although I don't believe it was a good idea to share my feelings on the matter with Nevah right now, I had to admit to myself that I enjoyed being claimed. I, of all people, was someone's man, a notion that continued to take me by surprise.

Chapter Twenty

Primo

A week later and not one attack was launched against my life. There was one subtle change I made that transitioned me from the most hunted man in St. Louis to one of the most watched.

The hunters lurked. They were still watching but not attacking. It was like the one who hired them made them take a time out. But the hired guns weren't who I truly wanted, I wanted the one who hired them, the one pulling the strings.

In my time of respite, I'd had to do the one thing I regretted doing the most. I forced myself to separate from Nevah. Whether I wanted to accept it or not, she was a part of the equation that dealt with me being hunted.

I needed to see if sending Nevah away would change the dynamics of my situation. It did, almost immediately. The implications alone were enough to make my men question my judgment. Not vocally, but in their actions. The need to know where I was keeping Nevah. The slight hesitation and questions when I gave them an order. The side eyes leveled at me when they thought I wasn't looking. I had never given them a reason to question my judgment.

It meant this hit out on me and the way I was handling it had shaken the foundation of our strong front. In order to maintain the order and respect I earned, I needed to put an end to this situation by any means necessary.

The separation between me and Nevah hadn't been easy for either of us despite me having a few questions lingering in the back of my mind. Nevah had fought like hell to stay at my side even after all she experienced from being connected to me. Her actions with me in the face of danger, in the face of death itself, reminded me why I should continue to trust her.

"They took the bait," Aurelio's voice came across loud and clear in my ear, dragging me back to my current reality.

"Good," I replied. Although I didn't see the tail Aurelio was referring to, I sensed them near. A deep steadying breath helped to clear more clutter from my mind and ready me for my next move.

I was on my way to Leandra's house, strolling through the streets like I didn't have multiple sets of killers waiting for a chance to snuff out my life. Truth was, I liked the attention more than I should have. It fed my ego and calmed the savage urges.

"Lenni. Umberto," I called after hitting their number.

"Yes."

"Capo."

They answered, Umberto's voice was lower indicating he was further away from the line. There was a spark of glee in their tone like they were hyped up on coffee at four in the afternoon.

"Do you have eyes on the eyes?" I questioned, already knowing the answer.

"Yes. The one who returned last night after they followed you is still here," Lenni confirmed.

"Be ready in a few minutes. The other one is following me now. I got a feeling they are going to try something today. They think I'm being careless due to the recent decrease in attempts on my life. If they do engage, I want to take them alive, if possible."

"Got it. See you soon," Lenni said before silence filled the line.

We tested Leandra's stalkers last night to see if they would make a move on me. They had. They tailed me for twenty minutes until I led them to exactly where I wanted them. I had left one of them watching a large apartment complex I drove into before hiding my car inside the garage of one of our old safehouses.

Since the men were unable to pinpoint where I had gone, they decided to split up. One sat at the complex and the other went back to put eyes on Leandra's place. Taking them alive would give us a chance to find out who hired them.

After confirmation that one was still watching the apartments, I made sure I was there to drive out so he would follow. I was itching for them to make a move, preferably one that would lead to who hired them.

While Nevah was away, I spent more time with Leandra. Assigning her odd jobs is what had kept her and her advances at bay. I also allowed her to accompany me on a few of my more tedious jobs.

She assumed my newfound interest had something to do with her and the relationship she thought we would start. With Nevah out of the picture, it made my interest in her that much more believable.

She never grew tired of asking me what happened to my new girlfriend, and I didn't get tired of giving her evasive answers like, 'we decided to take a break' or 'she needed a break.' The little smirk she flashed at my answers indicated what I thought she would assume, that our split was because of her.

As much as I hated deceiving Leandra, my interest in her had nothing to do with us and everything to do with finding out who was stalking her. Since Leandra was often associated with the DeLuca men, she was a means to an end. A way for my enemy to get more opportunities to destroy me and more DeLucas.

They had already used her, feigning an attack against her so that she would come running right to us. She had come to the club and met with Brizio and me, giving the hunters exactly what they wanted.

The others were careful after losing two men so soon after starting their quest. If they wanted me bad enough to go through Leandra to get me, I wasn't going to prolong their mission any longer than necessary. I needed to get these targets off my back even if it meant using myself as bait.

Earlier, I called Leandra and informed her that I would be taking her to her salon appointment today. She screamed so loud I'd had to remove the phone from my ear.

She must have been waiting at the door for my arrival. I was still pulling up the driveway and she was already out the front door and bouncing towards my car. All it would take is one wrong move and her tits would pop out of her top. One wrong turn and the jeans she painted on would rip.

We exchanged pleasant greetings when I walked around to open her door for her.

"Thank you Primo. You are such a gentleman," she purred at me. I endured her pressing her lips into my cheek longer than was necessary. I even left her blood red lipstick on my cheek for a few seconds before swiping it off.

Once she was inside, I cast a glance towards the gray Honda with the dark tent while returning to my side of the car. I could sense the men's eyes burning a hole in me.

An edgy tingle rolled up my spine after we pulled off. The Honda hadn't moved, and I no longer saw the dark blue Jeep that had followed me from the apartment complex.

Distracted, I answered Leandra's questions about how I was doing, my day, and so forth with one and two word phrases. After some of her energy died, the cab of the car grew silent. There was nothing I could think to talk to her about, so I just drove and kept an eye out for trouble.

I acknowledged Umberto and Lenni with a flick of the eye while driving past them. Leandra turned in the seat to watch them until their car disappeared from her view.

After a long pause, I sensed her eyes on me.

"So this is what it's always going to be like, being with you? All work and no play?" She questioned, turning in the passenger seat to get a better look at my face.

"You wanted this, advocated for it when I tried to warn you that I didn't have time for much outside of trying to run this city."

She tossed a deadly side eye at me and I knew exactly what she fought not to say. That I had found time for Nevah. I ignored her narrowed eyes.

"I'm in a tough position right now, fighting to stay alive while attempting to find out who's trying to kill me. Weren't you the one that said, and I quote, *"I'll be there for you if you need me, like a relationship of convenience."* Well, you're up. It's your time to be there for me and right now I need you to help me stay alive long enough to…"

I left the sentence open. I couldn't even force myself to say the lie out loud. I didn't want her and didn't understand how she didn't see it, sense it even. How long was I going to be able to lead her on before she figured out that I was using her to find my enemy?

I drove to the salon on Pine and North 10th Street preparing to drop her off at her appointment. I spotted the dark colored Jeep trailing us at least five miles back.

Leandra leaned over and caught me with another lingering kiss on the cheek, since my attention was on the vehicle.

"Call me when you're ready," I told her, forcing a smile to touch my lips and stay. She climbed out of the car with a little extra pep in her step glancing back at me grinning.

I expected the Jeep to approach, but I didn't expect them to do it in such a public place. I believe they were going to get things started right here on the street in front of the salon.

With sheer will of mind, I tried to force the idea into Leandra's head to walk faster. Although I was using her, it didn't mean I wanted her caught in the middle of someone's attempt to execute me.

The Jeep crept along the road, nearing me from the rear. Only a shadow of the man could be seen through the dark tint of the windshield. Leandra had nearly cleared the walkway that led to the entrance of the building.

She reached for the door but stopped and tossed up her hands as if frustrated before turning back in my direction. My eyes zoomed in on her keys, left sitting in the passenger seat.

Fuck!

Shit was about to get ugly, and she was walking right back into the mess. The Jeep was feet away at this point, sealing Leandra's fate. I leaned over and slung the passenger side door open.

"Run! Get in! We got company. Bad company!" I yelled, my urgent tone causing her to take up a wobbly jog in those heels. She glanced up and her wide eyes and gaped mouth had me whipping my neck around.

Gun!

The asshole had rolled down his passenger side window, and the gleam of shiny metal was all I saw reflecting off the July sun.

Leandra dived into the front seat a millisecond before the first bullets impacted the car, sounding like rocks being thrown against it. I drove off in a mad dash with one of her legs still hanging out of the door. Bullets pelted my side of the car, the bulletproofing shielding us from being sprayed with hot metal.

Leandra managed to pull herself inside and slammed the door shut before I gave the driver's side wheels a serious test of their durability. I cut off the Jeep at its attempt to ram my side of the car and took the next left on screeching tires.

Ducking low, Leandra held her chest with one hand and the nails of her other hand dug into the dash, her knuckles white. For a while, I suspected her of working with the guys who were watching her in an attempt to throw us off by having us think she had stalkers.

Based on the level of fear racing through her and the fact that she too was being shot at, I'd venture to say that she was nothing more than a means to my end, collateral damage.

I drove like NASCAR was paying me. It was time I led the man following me to church, one I frequented for reasons other than bible study.

No less than ten minutes later, we turned into the St. Andrew's catholic church's parking lot. Leandra's mouth flew open, head tilted and wide eyes locked on me.

I drove around the back, going way too fast in a parking lot, so I slowed enough to turn the bend around the back of the building. The sharp turn jerked us sideways. My tail, lured by the idea of ending my life, followed.

I kept going, passing the small parking area behind the church before cutting through the narrow passage cut between the burial plots in the vast graveyard.

We headed for the mortuary manager's little brick building sitting like a monumental beacon in the center of the graveyard. Another sharp turn took us close to the back of the building.

When my car was perfectly aligned with the right area behind the smaller building, I clicked the remote in my pocket. All I needed the man behind me to do was keep driving.

When the shriek of black chasing me made a sharp turn, determined to chase me down, the two tons of metal just dropped. And the grassy ground above the area rolled back into place, trapping the man inside a vehicle sized grave.

I kept driving, ignoring Leandra's wild-eyed gaze. I couldn't help wondering what the man thought of driving himself into a grave large enough to swallow his vehicle. If we didn't have a need for information, we could just leave him down there to suffocate. The man was literally stuck inside a car sized casket.

"Primo," Leandra's breathless voice called. "What the hell was that? We. Just…They…"

"A trap," I replied to her stammering words. "You've had a tail on you since the night you were attacked. Umberto and Lenni have been watching like I told you they would. But, they have also been watching the men who were watching you to make sure they didn't hurt you."

She cocked a squinting gaze in my direction, but her eyes were pinned on the ceiling above my head. I could almost see the vast number of questions and scenarios running through her mind.

"I suspected they were watching you to get to me. Brizio confirmed it. We set a plan in motion. I had no intention of getting you stuck in this today, but here we are."

"What are you going to do?" she questioned. "To them?" she was breathing like she'd been running, hopped up on adrenaline from the situation.

I never let everyone know all the secrets I harbored where it concerned catching, trapping, and killing prey. Leandra was never supposed to see what she just saw.

I rolled to a stop and turned the vehicle off once we were back in the large front parking lot of the church. A few cars were scattered throughout the lot, but not enough to be concerned about.

I handed Leandra the keys and finally answered her question.

"You don't want to know what I'm about to do to them. But I can promise you this. I'll find out once and for all who put a contract out on me."

She swallowed hard and took the keys.

"Are there more of them watching me? Is it okay for me to go back home?"

I nodded and glanced up in time to see Lenni and Umberto pulling into the church's parking lot and heading around the back.

"You should be okay, but…" I handed her a piece of torn paper I pulled from my pocket. "Go to that address and stay there until I call you."

She caught my arm, stopping me when I reached to push the door open. Her face was pinched in frustration.

"Were you just using me to get to who wants you dead? Did we ever have a chance? Are you still with…her?"

"I wasn't just using you," I told her, purposely making a vague statement to spare her feelings. However, I knew she knew the truth based on the defeated glint in her gaze. I hopped out.

Leandra sat with the car running. I sensed her heated stare on me until she decided to drive away.

She didn't need to know anything about Nevah. She already knew too much about the church grounds. She was supposed to be inside the salon right now, not wondering about the plans I had set into motion.

Chapter Twenty-one

Primo

Umberto's blacked out Audi was parked in the small lot outside the small mortuary office, which meant he and Lenni had already unloaded their package and were waiting for me.

I scanned the area, taking in hundreds of gravesites, some dating back more than a hundred-twenty years. The prickly feeling riding my bones signified an ominous energy stirring in the air. The dead weren't resting in peace like they'd been promised all their living lives.

My cousin Romigi made sure he'd coordinated to keep all traffic away from the graveyard today, a task much harder than one would assume as some people worshiped the dead. There were also three burials we were holding up. However, for the amount of money they were likely paid the dead themselves didn't mind the extra wait time.

Thankfully, Romigi had transplanted maple trees years ago that were strategically located throughout the graveyard and outside the building. The tree at the rear of the large grave site provided cover from distant eyes at the church. It also provided a measure of cover from whatever was trapped and itching to crawl out of that hole.

A quick glance around showed me I was in the clear to carry out my mission. The vast view over the graves showed the massive church in the distance as the backdrop.

As much as I hated to mess up my suit, I dropped into a prone position and took up a good defensive posture. The thick grass under the tree was plush enough to act as a natural blanket. The ground over the top of the gravesite was also grass covered, allowing it to blend into the landscape.

I extracted the little remote from my inner jacket pocket. Aiming it at the area where the back of the Jeep should be which was near the location of the remote's receiver. I pressed the tiny silver button and the door's motor hummed with life. I steadied my aim while the door slid to a slow grinding opening.

Half way open, I glimpsed the back of the Jeep. The automatic lights illuminated the hole. The vehicle was still running like the driver was aiming to stroll his way through the ground like a mole. Didn't he know about carbon monoxide poisoning? Or was that his goal, to die before we got to him?

A few more agonizingly slow seconds and...

Tap! Tap!

The silenced shots from the assassin's pistol struck the tree high above me. He peeked his head out just long enough to fire off a few more rounds. If I didn't want him alive, he'd be dead.

"You can voluntarily climb out of that hole, or I can come down there and get you. But, I will give you fair warning. If I have to drag your ass out of there, you are not going to like what I do to you afterwards."

"Fuck you and your plans!" The man yelled before releasing two more shots. His feet scraped against the metal flooring, the sounds bouncing around the tight space like a rat scurrying around inside a wall.

I picked up the remote and pressed the button that would seal this asshole back inside that hole. When it was a third of the way closed, the man peeked his head out again, only to stare into the barrel of my gun before he dropped back down.

Water, fire, and gas were my choices on the remote. I pushed the gas button and waited. I loved playing with Romigi's toys. They were just as deadly and savagely appropriate as mine were.

Romigi and I enjoyed a friendly contest, sometimes waging bets on who could come up with the most interesting contraptions to aid in our quest to stop our enemy and maintain order by DeLuca standards.

After no more than a minute's wait, I pressed the button to re-open the gravesite. I stood and dusted myself off before strolling over to peek inside.

The man was slumped beside the Jeep's driver's side rear tire, sleeping like a well-fed baby.

Once my gun was secured in its holster under my jacket, I jumped into the hole to retrieve my catch.

I suggested to Romigi a better way of retrieving from this hole and he loved my ideas, but our leisure time in the past few years was nonexistent. Like me, Romigi preferred setting up his own traps. He was also very particular about who he let see his toys.

It took me five minutes to heft the heavy ass sleeping man out of the hole, using the dented hood of his jeep to give me a boost.

Thankfully, the coast remained clear of any of the churchgoers who treated the graveyard like it was a temporary retreat from life. After closing the hole and giving the area a once over, I slung the man over my shoulder, and took off for the front of the building.

I snatched the front door open and stepped inside. The office space inside the building was large enough for a sitting area, desk and computer equipment, and a small kitchenette.

Umberto and Lenni stood against the front of the desk and was engaged in a game of rock paper scissors before I walked in. They shot up at the sight of me with the man hanging limp across my shoulder. Before they could offer me a hand, I tipped forward and let the man hit the floor.

The hard impact with the floor knocked the man out of his stupor. He grunted, his face squinted in pain and confusion. His eyes darted around the room as quickly as his neck could turn his swiveling head.

"What the fuck..."

I cut him off.

"Get up and let that couch grab your ass or I'll be happy to give you a one way ticket to your maker."

The man complied, dragging his body up and falling onto the couch next to his friend. Blood still oozed from the head wound he must have suffered when he drove his Jeep into the hole.

The other man looked like the brothers had tossed him in a cage with a man-eating lion. They had obviously had a little fun with him based on the bruises painting his face and his badly disheveled and torn clothing.

When the door was pulled open, Romigi stood in the open door in his dark cleric's robes. Two large white crosses sat high on either side of his chest and stood out against the black cloth. The crisp white of his collar gleamed just as bright as those crosses.

Romigi had a supernatural presence that would either creep you out or intrigue you. His unblinking gaze was fixed on our prey, and with that bible tucked against his chest, he could put the fear of God in someone with only a look.

Umberto and Lenni stared in wide-eyed anticipation. They were aware that Romigi put in work on behalf of the family, but they'd never had the privilege of seeing him in action.

Romigi finally stepped inside, his gaze lifting from the men to meet mine.

"Primo, my favorite cousin," he greeted, reaching his hand out to shake mine.

"Father Romigi," I greeted, addressing him by the proper name used in his official church capacity.

"Umberto. Lenni," he said, acknowledging them with a perceptive nod and smile.

"Father Romigi," they said in unison. Although they showed him respect, straightening their postures and with the slight bow of their heads, it was being overshadowed by the deep well of intrigue pouring from their upturned eyes.

Many in the community came to Romigi for spiritual guidance, upliftment, and help when they were down on their luck. They never considered that his last name gave him a different set of job duties. He may have been a spiritual advisor to most and was good at his job, but his bloodline made him a savage.

He stepped in front of the men, glancing down at them with an unreadable expression on his face. At thirty-five he'd made his mark on the community as well as earned a tremendous amount of respect among the Catholic church hierarchy.

"Are you the fallen?" he asked the men, who glared at him like they were one breath from hopping up to slap him in the face. His clean shaven and fresh faced appearance would make one think he was an imposter. Therefore, the men didn't hold any respect for Romigi and eyed him from head to toe, no doubt wondering if he was really a priest.

"Let me pray for you, my children."

His voice, like himself, was so calm and unassuming it was difficult for me to see him as anything other than a priest.

Romigi flipped the bible open and held it out to the men palmed in one of his hands. One took a look at the bible and glared up at Romigi with death flashing in his gaze. The other hawked up a big wad of spit, aimed, and painted the bible with his spit.

"Fuck you, your prayers, and that bible," he snarled, his lips pulled back like a wild dog's. Now, I understood why that one already carried bruises upside his head from Umberto and Lenni.

Romigi didn't say anything. He simply reached into his robe and extracted a snow white cloth. He shook the cloth out with one quick flick, unfolding it before he started cleaning the bible. His eyes would lift to the man every few seconds until he was satisfied with the cleanliness of the bible. His facial expression had never changed and gave away nothing. He placed the cloth back in his pocket, then...

Whoop!

Blood splatter flew across the floor from the mouth of the man who had just had the shit slapped out of him with Romigi's bible. He shook off the strike, closing his eyes, wiggling his jaw, and wiping at the blood dripping down his cheek.

The smug fucker still hadn't given up his contempt. It sat in the depth of his glare and shined through like the flames flaring from two torches. At least my enemy, whoever the hell they were, had employed a tough man in this one. He spit a wad of blood at Romigi's feet, along with a tooth that hit the wooden floor with a low, wet *clink*.

The cover of Romigi's bible was pitch black and many didn't give it too much attention. However, very few people knew that the material that covered the outer layer of Romigi's bible wasn't leather or cloth. It was made of shavings of the same type of lead as the tips of the flagrum that Jesus was beaten with. Handling the bible the wrong way would leave you cut and being hit with it as the man just had been, would rip your skin apart.

This man had gotten a lesson in what it meant to turn-the-other-cheek. The skin of his left cheek was missing and he had no other choice but to accept the outcome.

Romigi didn't wipe the man's blood or skin from the bible's outer covering like he had the spit. He repositioned the-good-book in his hand, laying it gently in his palm until he flipped to the page he wanted.

He extended the bible again, unbothered by the disdain covering both men's faces. His fatherly disposition was gone. The true savage in him sat just below his cool demeanor like that of a ghost; silent, watching, and waiting.

Umberto and Lenni side-eyed each other before the two returned their attention to Romigi, watching with rapt interest.

If the men had doubts about him being a priest before, they likely didn't know what to think of him now. I knew him well enough to know that he was seriously about to quote scripture to these men.

With a deeper look, I spotted the hint of reluctance and question in the spitting man's eyes. Was that a touch of fear I spotted as well?

The man I pulled from the Jeep kept flicking his eyes up and down from the bible to Romigi. The viciousness they had to possess in order to work in their profession had been knocked down a few pegs by the vibe in the room. They had no idea this was the quiet before the storm because I hadn't even laid hands on them yet.

"Each of you, place a hand atop this bible and I will bless you with the only peace you shall have for the rest of your lives."

The spitting man inhaled like he was preparing to spit on the bible again, but Romigi lifted one brow and allowed his gaze to burn with a flame borrowed from hell itself. The man, bleeding from his skinless cheek, turned his head away from Romigi and the bible. The other decided to place his hand atop the sacred white pages. He was wise to accept his fate and find spiritual guidance before it was too late.

"Bow your heads," he commanded. One man bowed along with me, Lenni, and Umberto. The missing cheek one, remained staring at the wall to his left.

"Like a sheep being led to the slaughter or a lamb that is silent before his shearers, he did not open his mouth."

He read from Isaiah 53:7 and continued. I knew more about the bible than many would believe. The passage pertained to this situation, specifically Romigi himself. It took me no time to figure out why he chose that specific passage. It wasn't for the reason one might assume.

Romigi's true nature was very often overlooked because of his profession. He was letting these men know that he was every bit the devil as every other man in this room, and he would be the one to ultimately lead them to their slaughter.

He allowed them a few minutes of peace and solitude, his head bowed while he continued to recite more scripture in a low, almost reassuring tone. He drew back and closed the bible with the hand he held it in. The resounding smack the pages made caused the one man to draw back his hand in a rush.

Romigi pulled up the wide arm of his robe and the keys attached to the thick bracelet around his wrist resembled keys that opened doors in an ancient castle. He was the only one with a set. He wore the keys around a copper bracelet and like someone with their pandora bracelet, he added a key for every new lock he needed to open.

He walked across the office with the silent grace of a cat and stopped at the four black metal file cabinets before bending at the one pushed up against the wall. He used one of the keys to open the bottom drawer.

Once inside the drawer, he punched in a series of numbers, the sequence of at least twenty, before an elongated beep sounded. The middle two file cabinets began to drop into the floor, the motor moving them sounded like the hum of an elevator.

Lenni and Umberto's expressions were that of two kids about to receive special gifts. I personally knew that they were about to see something that only a handful of DeLucas had witnessed.

The two file cabinets aligned perfectly with a set of stairs that would lead into the small prison that, like the keys, resembled a dungeon from an ancient castle.

Romigi preferred the old school methods of carrying out his family duties. Instead of incinerators, he dug graves. Instead of using a cleaning crew, he cleaned up his own scenes. Instead of neat head shots to take out an enemy, he held on to them and bestowed long-term punishments that ravaged a man's soul from his body while impressing upon them spiritual enlightenment.

One of his nicknames was Father Time because he didn't rush the death process unless it couldn't be helped. I admired Romigi's skills and slow precision but didn't have that kind of patience.

Umberto and Lenni grabbed each of the men by the arms when Romigi signaled us to follow him. The men fought the brothers, punching, kicking, and cursing. I didn't blame them for fighting. I would have done everything in my power to free myself of a situation like this one.

We entered the dark path, the steps barely illuminated by the light shining in from the office. The men continued to resist, fighting against the inevitable truth unfolding with every dark step the brothers dragged them down.

Romigi reached up and turned a knob that made the fire flickering in the wall sconce grow brighter, but it did very little to chase away the shadows. We continued our descent, Romigi leading, Umberto and Lenni with the men followed with loud clumpy steps, while I brought up the rear.

At the bottom of the stairs, a chilling breeze circled us, the bite of cold in direct contrast to the eighty-nine degree July heat outside.

Rock, stone, and steel. The walls, the floor, even the beds the prisoners slept on were hard and cold and carved into the walls like crypts. The room was a perfect circle with a large five-pointed star painted white in the center of the floor to stand out against the dim setting.

There were four small cells that circled the main floor like a small arena. Each room was aligned with a point of the star, the final point aimed at the stairs we descended. Three of the four cells housed men that Romigi was keeping here for one reason or another. I didn't ask and he didn't volunteer to tell me. One of the prisoners was groaning an agonizing cry so icy, it helped intensify the chill in the air.

I had my own dark prison of sorts to be concerned about. Besides, Romigi's set up, which usually had an audience of other prisoners, worked wonders on getting people to talk.

Lenni and Umberto managed to wrestle the men into the large slab of concrete the size and height of a bench, sitting inside the body of the star.

The men put up a good enough fight that Romigi was forced to lift his bible threateningly to keep them in check. I'm sure the men had concluded by now that a quick death was better than what they might get in this place.

Affixed to the back of the thick slab of concrete were shackles connected to chains the brothers used to cuff the men's hand behind their backs. Their feet were cuffed to the front of the slab.

I went over to one of the dark corners, where small, recessed areas like a closet sat on each side of the stairs. I pulled out a metal stand with wheels attached to the bottom and parked it in front of the men. I returned to the dark space to retrieve a small hard-covered briefcase filled with an impressive variety of gleaming cutting instruments.

I positioned the suitcase in front of the waiting men, who tracked every move I made. Umberto and Lenni, stood about four feet away next to Romigi, watching, waiting, anticipating.

Romigi and I had tortured enough people together that he usually had an idea of what I had in mind, if not, he got the picture soon enough.

Bending, I allowed my hands to run along the tops of the sharp instruments in the case while glancing up at the men, my eyes volleying between them.

"Who are you working for? Which DeLuca hired you to kill me?"

One swallowed, the other tilted his damaged cheek and chin up in stupid defiance. There was always one tough guy who volunteered himself to be the example that would inspire the others to talk.

I picked up one of the smallest instruments from the collection, a shiny scalpel that gleaned against the dim lighting of the two sconces on either side of the space. The man who volunteered as tribute, leveled an angry glare at me when I pointed the scalpel at him.

Romigi stepped up and pushed the metal stand between the man's shackled feet, the heavy base of it built to fit perfectly between the man's feet. Did Romigi already have an idea of what I had in mind?

The tribute flashed me a quick side eye when he noticed the large metal hooks attached like branches to the thick metal pole, making the equipment resemble a coat rack.

Easy steps took me around the slab and kept every eye in the place, including those of the prisoners tracking my every move.

Once behind the tough guy, I reached down and adjusted the cuffs around his wrist, yanking them down and cuffing them to take some of the length from the chain, leaving the man no choice but to lie back at an odd angle.

Since his feet were shackled and pulled taunt against the metal holding them in place, he remained off balanced, wobbling atop the slab.

His friend stared, deathly still. His eyes were so riveted to the scene unfolding right before his eyes, he didn't appear to be breathing.

I reached over the smart mouthed one in front of me and sent the scalpel across his lower torso region in one long slash. The material of his shirt gaped open exposing his stomach before he realized he was cut. He gaped down at himself, along with everyone else.

My goal was to cut away his clothing, not caring if he was cut in the process. Seeing that I accomplished my goal without cutting him was an impressive task that had me wanting to practice until I perfected the move.

However, I pulled at the top half of his shirt and kept cutting until it was easily ripped from his body. The man weaved and wobbled but his attempts to straighten himself out were useless.

I took my time walking back around the slab to the front of the man who still hadn't lost his defiant edge.

Good.

I fought a smirk. He wanted to play big boy games and come for my life, now he was about to find out the price of coming for someone in a family he must have failed to research.

Romigi shoved the metal stand as close as he could get it to the man until the base touched the concrete slab the man sat atop.

"What the fuck are you about to do, you sick fuck?" he questioned, spitting his words at Romigi before he growled at me baring teeth.

"About to show you what happens when you come for a DeLuca and miss. We are also about to get you…" I aimed my head at his friend without dropping my gaze from his blazing one. "...to get him to tell us who hired you."

"I'm not a fucking rat. I'll never talk. No matter what you do," the man sneered. "And neither will he," he continued, speaking for the other man who was going to break faster than a rotten egg.

I enjoyed the rough edge of the man's aggression. Part of me was proud he wasn't a wimp. Part was glad he would make my job of ripping him apart easy. And part of me was holding in the sick pleasure I would get from turning that defiant attitude into one of sheer horror.

Distracted by Romigi opening his bible again, he didn't see me make the second quick slash across his stomach, right above his navel.

When the pain registered, his head shot down and his eyes widened at the sight of blood pouring from the four inch gash that opened to a sizable hole when he moved. Instincts made him yank his hands up in an attempt to cover the area, but his sharp movement didn't do anything but make his blood spill faster.

"Fuck you!" he yelled, sneering at me. "And you," he said glaring in Romigi's direction.

"And you two psycho fucks too," he spat in Umberto and Lenni's direction. They remained silent and observing, learning tactics I was sure they would use later.

After bending to retrieve a surgical glove from the briefcase on the floor. I snapped it onto my right hand with quick precision like a doctor preparing for surgery.

The man's legs and arms flailed uselessly against the chains and shackles stopping him from breaking free. He wobbled, teetering on his ass while blood gushed in spurts and spilled down his pale stomach.

I bent forward, reaching my hand towards his stomach and dodged a wad of spit. I glanced up at his tightly pinched, pain drenched face.

"You have one more time to spit, and I'll put something in your mouth that you will never be able to get out."

He narrowed his eyes at me without saying a word. I jerked back in the nick of time, my reflexes helping me clear the area he tried to send his knee. I bet his ankles were thanking him for that move.

I didn't even have to ask, Romigi was behind the man in a flash, placing the closed bible over his mouth and yanking him back so hard his legs kicked up and clinked hard against the chain keeping them shackled to the slab.

The man cursed up a storm and Romigi was careful not to cover his eyes, wanting him to see every action. I placed my gloved fingers against the man's wound and smiled at his wide gaping eyes.

"What the 'uk doin'?" He tried to talk around the bible that I knew was ripping skin off his lips.

When I shoved my fingers into the opening of his wound, he screamed, the guttural sound, though muffled by the bible, was still loud enough to rattle the metal on the cells. Romigi removed his bible and allowed the man's loud shouts to liven up the dank dungeon, sensing he was in too much pain to launch another attack.

The friend released a choking gasp, when I moved my fingers around inside the man, and shoved them in deeper. With most of my hand wiggling around the inside of his stomach region, his eyes started to roll to the back of his head and his shouts grew intense enough to knock dust from the ceiling and walls.

His muscles clenched so tight from his straining cries, the force pushed against my blood slicked fingers and made some squirt from the opening.

"My God," I think I heard his friend mutter, his eyes floating saucers in his head. The dim lighting in the room made the scene much more ominous and intensified the senses, adding to the wet, fleshy sounds bouncing off the walls and the pungent smell that packed a punch of a different kind.

I wasn't going to stop my search until I found what I was looking for or heard what I was waiting to hear.

"Who do you work for?" I questioned, not looking at the one sucking in air like his lungs had collapsed, but the friend who was sweating despite the chill that coveted this space. The man shook his head.

"I promise you. I don't know. But, our friend Broady, he…"

He paused to breathe or keep down his lunch, I didn't know and didn't care. He gave up a name and was preparing to spill his guts without my help.

"You already killed Broady when he tried to use the woman to set you up at the safe house. He was the one who put us on to this job. I think he may have had contact with the one you're looking for."

So the ones who took Nevah hostage at the safe house belonged to this endangered group. These were the unaccounted for ones that Brizio had mentioned.

The unmerciful cursing and yelling the man was doing continued as did my fingers pushing aside and raking across internal organs.

"That's not good enough," I told the friend. "Somebody knows something more."

With his lips looking like two overripe plums, my loud mouthed tribute attempted to spit out a few choking words.

"It was your family…who…who hired us to kill you," he said coughing and blowing out rapid breaths in an attempt to lessen the pain shooting through him.

"Did someone tell you to say it was a DeLuca? Can you name the DeLuca who hired you?"

With my middle finger wrapped around his small intestine now, I pulled, slowly allowing him to see his own bowels being extracted.

His yells hit a decibel I didn't know existed. The pain, the sight, the smell that started to fill the room had him screaming now and unwilling to move. When I had about a foot of his gut stretched out into the air, I continued to pull.

"Damn."

"Holy fuck."

Umberto and Lenni, uttered. They were closer now, a few feet behind my back. Their blood thirsty nature had them unwilling to miss a thing even as they coughed from the thick stench permeating the space.

"Sorry, father Romigi," Lenni said when Romigi tossed an authoritative glance in his direction, I presume for using holy and fuck in the same breath.

Romigi knew better than to discipline me for cursing. I told him cursing was one of the few ways I exercised my demons.

By the time I stopped pulling, about a foot and a half of the man's intestines were stretched out. I looped them over the first metal hook on the medieval coat rack between his legs to ensure he kept an eye on his personal property.

I didn't hear a sound from the other prisoners in the cells who likely assumed they were getting a sneak peek of their fates.

The unstuffed man sipped air in rapid pants. Sweat dripped from him like water while Romigi recited words from the book of Revelation, his tone smooth like he was soothing one of his troubled flock. Although he had the bible open for effect, he never stopped studying the men.

"He will wipe away every tear from your eyes, and death shall be no more, neither shall there be mourning, nor crying, nor pain anymore, for the former things have passed away."

Romigi's words were calm and purposeful like he belonged on a commercial to promote meditation. I guess he thought his spiritual words soothed men in times of torture. I didn't have the heart to tell him, he wasn't doing shit but scaring more hell into the damned ones he preached to when they were confronted by death.

I focused my attention on the one in front of me, snapping my fingers to get his attention off his protruding intestines, if only for a few seconds.

"De-de-escription…" was all the man could get out before his blood dripping guts drew his attention.

"Please," rushed out his mouth.

"Were you told to say it was a DeLuca who hired you? Can you positively say, without a doubt, that it was a DeLuca who hired you?"

"We never met the person. We never met them," the friend said, his words rushed and his eyes begging for his friend's mercy.

"Fucking put-put-put me out of my misery," the whimpering one said, begging now that he had been humbled.

"This is nowhere near the misery I could make you feel. I could leave you here until your guts dry up and your stomach backs up and feeds you the food you ate last week. I'm being nice because I don't want you to pass out before you tell me what I need to know. Now, you were saying something about a description."

"My man said...it was, it was... a woman..." he said, his eyes fluttering and his body lulling to the side. He snapped his eyes open and jerked back to the present, his wide eyes glazed. Fear had a tight grip now that he realized death was only a breath away.

Romigi flipped a page in his bible, the sound, though low on the auditory scale, was enough to drag the man's attention back to what he was saying.

"It was a woman who hired us. He claims she was black, but we-we ne-never saw anyone." He paused, swallowing hard. All of his energy had been pulled right out of him, making it hard for him to keep his head lifted.

"We got our instructions and were paid electronically," the friend added, finishing for him. His wide eyes, unblinking and filled with fear, were on his friends' exposed intestines. The way he gulped and the paleness of his skin suggested he was about to throw up any second.

"I believe the plan was to make it look like one of the other families had set it all up. I think she's trying to start a war within your family as well as between the families."

All eyes were on me now. My mysterious new girl-friend was the number one suspect in their heads now. My uncharacteristic behavior with her from the start had al-ways been a question my men were trying to find an answer to behind my back.

I shook my head even as I thought it. There was no way Nevah would set me up like this.

Fuck what this man was saying. I'd had Nevah's background thoroughly checked out. Besides, she had nothing to gain from wanting me dead. Nothing to gain by starting a war.

Romigi moved, standing beside me now. He was studying every nuance of the men and breaking it down like he did scripture.

My gaze sat on the one who quieted, his harsh breaths the only sound filling up the space. His eyes hung heavy in his lulling head. His body shook from exhaustion or shock. I couldn't tell.

"Description," I said, eyeing him with enough dis-dain that he visibly shivered. The crazy mother fucker, shook his head, unwilling to give up what he knew.

"Awww!" The gutless one screamed, more like squealed, when Romigi kicked the metal stand about an-other foot back, ripping out more of his intestines. The sound of his inside being yanked out sent rippling waves of fear into the other man.

The yelling went quiet, so suddenly it had Lenni and Umberto glancing over my shoulder and literally breathing down my neck to see if he was dead. His body hung lopsided. The foot shackles kept his legs anchored to the concrete below while his top half fell completely back and dragged out another foot of gut. A larger organ pushed at the hole, threatening to break free.

"Broady said she was a really pretty black chick. Said her name was Heaven or something. That's all I know. I never saw her. That's all he told us after giving us a long speech about not trusting women."

His eyes flicked to his friend and back to me in a flash. When I shot a quick glance at Romigi, he nodded once, letting me know that this man fully believed what he was saying.

Now, it was up to me to determine if I had been lied to, or if I were in fact being deceived by the one person I believed I could trust. I didn't give my trust easily, but once I gave it to someone, I was never sorry for the decision. Was it possible my judgment, I once thought ironclad, had failed me where it concerned Nevah?

"I need to figure some shit out," I told Romigi, handing him the blade. He handed me a set of keys before I stepped off.

"Capo, you need us?" Umberto called after me, him and Lenni taking steps to follow me.

"Stay with Romigi, I may need you for another detail later."

My thoughts were firing off so fast, they were playing target practice with my mind. I was halfway up the stairs, when I heard, "For I am the Lord, your God, who takes hold of your right hand and says to you, Do not fear, I will help you."

"Isaiah 41:13," I said under my breath. Romigi was going to help them all right. Help them right down to the gates of hell.

The sound of tortured screams didn't even entice me to go back to witness what Romigi was down there teaching Lenni and Umberto.

I had a mystery that needed to be solved before I ended up making a decision I couldn't take back.

"Aurelio," I called into my phone when the line clicked on. I wasn't even sure when I dialed his number.

"Yes," he answered before a loud thump, and a straining male voice sounded, letting me know that someone was on the business end of one of his fists.

"I have a very important mission for you," was all I said before clicking off.

Chapter Twenty-two

Nevah

A week had flown by, and Primo was in the wind, giving minimal phone conversations and no in-person interactions. It was like he had quit on us cold turkey after I finally allowed myself to fall for him. Whatever our lives were before we connected didn't matter anymore because he was who I knew I wanted now.

My temporary home was a penthouse suite that he chose and paid for in Mt. Vernon, Illinois, about an hour away from St. Louis. The boredom was going to kill me faster than being the girlfriend of a mob boss.

When I could take no more, and after dodging calls and telling lies to my friends about why they couldn't see me, I caved. I called Tracy and Maya and invited them to join me a few towns over from where I was located.

I waited until we were all liquored up before hitting them with my major bombshell. I also ordered a VIP booth to give us a semblance of privacy.

"I'm dating someone," I blurted.

The soft music playing, people's muffled conversations, and all other background noises faded out. The scene around us appeared to temporarily pause to spotlight the two sets of wide, questioning eyes that were set on me.

I sipped from my margarita, pretending like I wasn't being crushed under the anticipation spewing from their waiting gazes.

Tracy slapped the fire from my forearm, making me jump and spill some of my drink that I paid for with the credit card my fiancé had gifted me before leaving.

"Are you going to tell us who the fuck you're dating, or are we going to have to tie your secret-keeping ass down and torture it out of you?" Maya questioned with a fixed gaze and set jaw.

"He's probably not someone either of you would approve of me dating. He's kind of dangerous but he treats me really well."

"How long have you been dating this guy?" Tracy asked, flashing me the eye squint that said I better not lie.

"I met him at the club a few weeks ago when we were there."

They snatched their heads back in disbelief.

"That's why your fast ass wanted to leave so soon after we arrived. You could have told us you were sneaking off with a man. Who the hell is this miracle worker who had you ditching your friends these past few weeks?"

Although I couldn't disclose everything, I decided to share at least his identity.

"His name is Primo DeLuca."

Maya choked so hard on the sip of drink she took that Tracy slapped her on the back, the hard licks sounding off despite the noise of the other diners trickling into our space. Although she was taking care of Maya, her hand rubbing gently up and down her back, Tracy's wide gaze was pinned on my face.

"It happened by accident. I was searching for Maya and the guy she walked away with and sort of just ran into him when I peeked into one of the back offices. We talked and hit it off."

It wasn't a total lie.

The sound of crickets chirping might as well have been going off because my friends were speechless. There were no snappy comments about my mental state lobbed at me. Neither of their hands were pressed against my forehead to see if I was feverish. They were good old-fashioned shocked. So much so their frozen state caused me to wave a hand in front of their faces to wake them.

"You're serious?" Tracy finally questioned, her voice a harsh whisper. I didn't have to question if they knew who Primo was because their expressions said it all.

"We are not together at the moment because he's taking care of a family problem."

Tracy visibly swallowed while Maya hit me with another unblinking stare.

"Umm," Tracy dragged out, attempting to gather her thoughts, "once you're in one of those kinds of families, you can't get out of it, right?"

Maya shook her head at Tracy like she was the resident expert on mob life.

"That's not true. The men date, dump, and marry whoever they want. However, they are selective about the women they choose. It's usually women who are in similar families."

Maya flashed me an expression of mixed emotions, fear being the most prominent.

"Is this a relationship you want?" Maya questioned. Deep creases of worry were stretched across her forehead. She didn't give me a chance to answer.

"Some of those men *take* whatever they want, and it's my fault if you are stuck. If you hadn't been looking for me, you wouldn't be in this situation, hiding out and waiting until he *fixes* what I'm guessing is a dangerous situation since he obviously doesn't want you anywhere near it."

They had managed to piece together my situation without me having to water down why me and Primo were separated at the moment.

"I'm not being forced into this situation," I reassured them. "At first, I was against us having a relationship, but after spending some time around him, I honestly believe we can make it work."

You could have heard a pin falling through the air. They were used to me being the I-don't-give-a-damn-about-a-relationship friend. My candidness was also a way to get them comfortable with the idea that I was now tied to the mob if they wanted to remain friends.

It had taken many hours of long and hard reflection on how being with Primo could change the dynamic of our friendship. And I didn't have the heart to tell them that I virtually had no way out of my situation from the beginning.

"I'd certainly understand if you guys would want to keep your distance. I don't want…"

Tracy lifted a hand, cutting me off.

"I know what you're about to say, and you can chill with that shit. We are your girls, and I don't care who you're dating. It's not going to stop me from being your friend. Do I want you with someone a little more...safe? Shit, yes. But we are all placed in certain situations for reasons we may never understand. The house me and my kids live in was bought with drug money. We all know my husband wasn't always a legit business man. If you and that fine ass Primo DeLuca are meant to be, his job and who his family is don't matter."

"What she said," Maya said with a big grin on her face. "Here we are trying to force you down random men's throats, and you are dating one of the finest men in the damn city."

It pleased me that they didn't look at me with pitying expressions.

"Thank you. I appreciate you ladies wanting to keep me, but my life may become a lot more complicated than me hanging out in a hotel," I said, eyeing each of them. And although Primo didn't mention it, I was sure he had multiple sets of eyes on me—even now while I was hanging out with my friends.

"I know you can't disclose family secrets or anything, but if he said he needs to work something out, that means he's probably planning on killing people, right?" Maya questioned with intrigue shining in her gaze rather than fear or apprehension.

I didn't give an answer but allowed my eyes to rest on hers until she dropped them. All they saw was their good-natured friend who worked too much, volunteered at a nursing home, and was taking care of a mother that had never given a damn about her. They hadn't thought back yet to how we had all grown up.

"How's the dick? That man, although I've only seen his elusive ass once, looks like he could put it down," came Maya's question and comment that I should have expected. I was unaware that I was smiling at her crass question until two sets of approving eyes caught my attention.

"That damn good, huh? He got any more brothers? My poor pussy is starving, and if there is one thing I know, the more dangerous a man is, the more he knows how to lay the smack down in the bedroom. It's like the danger enhances their instincts, especially their sexual instincts."

I shook my head at Maya, who high-fived Tracy.

"Facts!" Tracy added.

We drank until my tongue went numb and laughed about the good ole days of college. I dodged most of their questions about Primo, fearing I'd said too much already.

"I need to go to the little girl's room," Maya announced, before taking a big gulp of her fourth or fifth drink.

Standing she walked away, her steps solid and strong in those heels even though I knew she was feeling the effects of the alcohol.

There was no need to whisper, but I did so now, leaning closer to Tracy.

"How is she? Really?"

The alcohol infused glee that was on her face dropped.

"She's still grieving and in doing so, making questionable decisions. Before her brother she hooked up, but now it's like she's on an expedition, running through men like they are nothing more than a temporary fix to a long-term problem. Like drugs," Tracy said, shaking her head.

"She's not still trying to solve her brother's case on her own is she?"

Thankfully, Tracy shook her head. "No, I think she's chilled with it for now. She..."

Tracy's abrupt stop let me know that Maya was on the way back. I was worried about her, and at times, had no idea how to help her other than being there for her.

Maya dropped back into her seat and continued where she'd left off, picking up her drink and sipping. An odd silence filled the space, but when we all glanced up at each other, we couldn't help cracking silly smiles.

"It's getting late. I don't want to stay out too late considering the new dynamics of my life."

Tracy's face crinkled. "Don't you mean reintroduction? We grew up in The Grind. If you had never seen a hood in your life, I think you would have packed up and run by now."

Maya nodded, and I could sense her taking a stroll down memory lane based on the far-off stare that projected like she was looking right through me.

"We might have all found a way out of the hood, but the lessons remain inside each of us. We don't run from a fight because we weren't raised that way. We don't take shit from anyone because we weren't taught to."

Maya sounded like the poster child for hood-raised kids. We had all faced our fair share of danger growing up. Tracy was shot in her lower back at fifteen. At twelve, I was stabbed in my left side and later, at seventeen, trapped in the car with one of my boyfriends while he was being chased by cops with half a kilo of coke in the car with us. I had managed to open the door and let the coke spill out before he was caught. We, as a group, had seen enough bodies to start our own morbid gallery of death scene portraits.

"Don't ever think that we would walk out on our friendship because your guy is not one of those squares that I like to take advantage of," Maya stated, her tone matter of fact.

They nodded in agreement, the sight making my eyes sting with the tears I fought to hold back.

"If that big, fine ass man of yours is ever in trouble, my advice to you is to help him in the safest way possible of course. If you ever need a little help from me, I'm game," Maya stated, and I believed her. However, I shook my head. Just because I was back in *the life*, it didn't mean they were coming with me.

"You ladies being here for me is all I need. Besides, I've seen Primo in action, and I don't think he's going to need my lightweight help."

An hour later, we hugged for what felt like an hour before they finally decided to release me. They were too drunk to drive home and opted to share a hotel suite across the street from the restaurant. Knowing they were safe I was content enough to make my way to the Uber I secured before waving one last reluctant good-bye.

Chapter Twenty-three

Nevah

The ride back to my suite was a silent one. I wasn't sure what type of vibe I was giving off, but the Uber driver remained silent, only looking up to glance in the dark rearview mirror every once and a while. It was like he sensed that I needed to think.

Like always, I texted my friends as soon as my ride pulled up to the front of my hotel's entrance. I climbed out of the car, the dark balmy night air landing like an unwanted touch. My short walk to the hotel's lobby doors was like trudging through a thick fog I couldn't see.

Once inside, the busy atmosphere brought back a sense of normality. I returned a wave to the front desk attendant, who greeted me each time he noticed me. I wouldn't have been surprised if Primo was paying him to keep an eye on me.

My phone buzzed, and I answered on the first ring when I saw it was him.

"Hello."

"Hi. How are you? How'd your outing go with your friends?"

"It went well. They want to keep me," I said, laughing and forgoing reaching out to hit the up arrow on the elevator to continue my conversation with Primo.

"I…"

"You…"

We spoke at the same time.

"You first," I suggested.

"I'm close to finding out who initiated the contract on me and killed my men. Hopefully, we can reunite within the week."

"I can't wait. I miss you." The sentiment in my tone surprised me as much as I believed it did Primo, who went silent.

"I miss you too. Stay safe. I'll see you soon."

"Okay." My voice cracked before I hung up. Did he sound strange, or was it the distance that made him sound a bit off?

I climbed on to the elevator with my ex-husband on my mind for reason's I couldn't recall. Why were the horrible memories of him surfacing lately? Maya and Tracy didn't know all the details about that part of my life or the true history of who I had foolishly married right under their noses.

What would they think of me if they knew I killed the man I had secretly married when I was nineteen and a few days before we reached our first month of marriage? A black eye and cracked ribs were what I was gifted for not following his impossible orders, one which was not to see or talk to my friends anymore.

Maya and Tracy had asked about the older man I'd dated off and on for a year. They never liked him despite my not disclosing to them that he was an ex-con, drug dealer, and a thief. They didn't think twice about never having to see him again after I announced our breakup.

The thick, eerie feeling was back in the air on my elevator ride up to the seventeenth floor. I stepped off the elevator and turned in the opposite direction of my room towards the stairs. Why was my sixth sense for danger going haywire?

After stepping into and standing inside the entryway into the stairwell and scoping out my surroundings, I finally cast my strange sense of urgency aside and stepped with quick caution to my room. I was sure if anybody saw me at the moment, they would think I was too wasted to know what I was doing. I was letting my paranoia get the best of me.

The buzzer sounded, alerting that my key card had slid home. I sprang the door open and stepped inside. I closed the door and flipped the latch for extra protection. The deep sigh I released in the process of toeing my shoes off stopped.

Ding Dong!

My hand covered my heaving chest after I jumped about a mile high at the sound of the doorbell. I saw the doorbell each time I entered the room, but hearing it sound off had scared the shit out of me.

Now, I was so filled with tension, my mind kept contouring up bloody images of me getting shot through the eye when I peeked to see who was at the door.

"Calm," I muttered under my breath. If it was someone from the mob trying to kill me they wouldn't have rung the doorbell. They would have found a clever way to retrieve a key card.

At that notion, I ambled to the door and gave a quick peek. A deep sigh of relief swept through me at the sight.

After swinging the extra security lock open, I pulled the door open with a wide grin on my face.

"Aurelio," I said in greeting before sweeping my hand into the suite for him to enter. "Never thought I'd see you again so soon."

He stepped inside and headed for the small marble topped dining table. He positioned the white leather chairs so that I would be facing him directly before aiming his hand across the table. His serious expression and cold demeanor had me frozen in place.

Waiting, he allowed me time to gather myself. My legs felt heavy and my heart rate accelerated, but I inched closer and took the seat. Aurelio sat after I did and stared across the table at me.

"I'm going to ask you some questions and want you to answer them as quickly as you can and as honestly as you can."

I nodded. "Okay."

"You and Primo met under a set of unique circumstances, correct?"

"We met in his cousin's club," I told him, my voice dry, and emotionless.

"If you had met him, let's say, at a park jogging, would you have dated him?"

"No , but we're here now and I'm not sad about it. I believe we can be happy together."

He nodded, his expression unreadable. His eyes bore down on my face with quiet scrutiny.

"Aren't you afraid of Primo? Aren't you afraid that he's going to snap on you and set off some of that savage rage, I know you've witnessed?"

"Why are you doing this Aurelio? Did Primo put you up to this?"

"Answer the question," he said, his tone remaining even, almost soothing, but his gaze pinned mine, unblinking. "Please."

"No. I'm not afraid of Primo. There is no circumstance in which I'd ever believe he would hurt me."

Again, a simple nod and unreadable expression.

"How do you feel about Primo's job as Capo of St. Louis for the DeLuca Crime family?"

I shrugged. This was starting to sound like an interrogation, something that may get Primo into trouble if I didn't watch what I said. My gaze did a quick scan of Aurelio. Was he wearing a wire?

"I don't know what a Capo is. Every DeLuca that I've met has not given me any reason to be afraid...until now."

He cracked his neck, the sound piercing through the room although it was muffled.

"Do you feel safe around Primo? How long do you think you can last in his world before you catch a stray bullet or someone aiming for him gets you?"

The questions were getting tiring now.

"I could have a heart attack and die right here at this table. To assume that being around Primo will get me killed is pointless."

I could have sworn I saw a smirk on Aurelio's face, but was it one of mockery? I was starting to feel like a criminal, like he knew something about me that I didn't want getting out. Did he know that I'd snapped and killed my husband? Was that what this line of questioning was leading up to? Did he think I was crazy enough to snap and try to kill Primo too? The questioning dragged on.

Ten minutes.

Fifteen.

I did my best to give vague and evasive answers. It was the ones pertaining to how I felt about Primo that I couldn't hide from. My emotions where it concerned my feelings for him wouldn't be silenced. I had fallen for him way too fast and that in itself was questionable among his family.

"Would you lie for Primo if you witnessed him kill someone in cold blood?" Aurelio asked.

All of the questions were suspect, but this particular one was a red flag for me. It sounded like something a detective or law enforcement would ask a suspect or accomplice to murder. Aurelio knew I was with Primo when he had committed murder. Now, he was trying to get me to admit it.

My eyes squinted into slits.

"He would never murder someone in cold blood."

It wasn't a lie. Primo would make sure the person was making an attempt on my life, his life, or at least guilty of committing some horrific act against his family or humanity.

The slits I squeezed my eyes into caused my face to pull into a tight grimace.

"I didn't take you for a snake, Aurelio. I'm usually a pretty good judge of character. I truly believed you were loyal to your family."

He didn't comment, simply sat there and observed my every move, twitch, and eyeblink. "Are you some type of double agent, trying to get me to say some foul shit about Primo, so you can make a case. Well, it's never going to happen. He's a reputable citizen who pays his taxes and minds his own damn business. You and your questions can take the quick way out of this suite by jumping off the balcony."

I stood.

"I'm done."

I didn't care if he was done or not. He looked up at me. His facial expression changed so many times, I didn't know what the hell to think. A sparkle of a smile flickered across his gaze and disappeared with the smooth quickness of a lightning strike. Had I imagined it? Was my mind conjuring up hope where there was none? Right now, all I wanted was for this interrogation to have been some type of family test that we could laugh at later.

Aurelio stood. His imposing body and towering height intimidated me, but I dared not show a hint of unease.

"Thank you," he said before tipping his head forward and stepping away. His steps were as silent as if he were walking on cotton versus a marble floor in those expensive loafers.

He pulled the door closed behind him, and I re-anchored the security lock.

"That was…weird," I muttered, standing at the door, lost, confused, and terrified.

Chapter Twenty-four

Nevah

Aurelio had been sent to test my loyalty, not only to the DeLuca family, but to Primo. This was the logical conclusion I forced myself to believe over all the other scenarios hammering their way into my brain.

If this was some sort of test, manufactured by Primo, I didn't blame him. I was a target by association and couldn't imagine what it was like being under the same amount of pressure as him. Pressure to lead. Pressure to survive. Pressure to track down a traitor within his own family.

I needed a deep meditation session, something to get my mind off of...everything. I allowed my body to melt into the expensive couch cushions before throwing my head back and aiming it at the vaulted ceiling.

Eyes closed I inhaled so deeply I could feel the stress preparing to seep out of me. Another long breath dragged a familiar scent into my lungs. One I caught a whiff of when I had walked in. Aurelio's sudden emergence made me forget about it.

My eyes popped open.

My head tilted.

That scent.

I sniffed the air and wrinkled my nose. It was like candy.

Licorice.

I jumped up off the couch like it was on fire and went for my purse when I remembered exactly when and where I had smelled the scent.

"Don't!" a voice called out from the darkness in the back of the suite at the same time I was reaching out for my purse. Just another foot and I could snatch it up and get my gun. I moved my hand, inching my arm closer, determined to get to my bag.

"Move one more inch and this room will have to be decommissioned so they could clean up your splattered brains."

Fuck!

The clicking drew closer, more specifically the clicking of heels against the floor before the light shining behind her blocked her face from my view.

"Leandra," I whispered.

"Toss the fucking purse and sit over there," she instructed, pointing at one of the two chairs at the small dining table me and Aurelio had just vacated.

This was the most eventful night of my life. The thought that it could be the last one of my life limped into my brain carrying with it every emotion I had just tried to banish from my mind.

My purse hit the floor and landed next to the couch before cautious steps inched me closer to the chair Leandra pointed out. My eyes were glued to the gun in her hand. There was no need to ask her why she was here or how she found me—she wanted Primo and would go to any lengths to have him.

Her eyes and body language when I spotted her with him at the restaurant told me that her desire for Primo was immeasurable. She came across as a bit stalkerish, especially when she bumped into my shoulder after leaving the table.

The wild glint in her eyes now said she was about to do something crazy.

I didn't take the seat but stood in place, staring at her with what I hoped was a droopy, sorry-eyed expression. I may have been giving off more of a vibe that spilled seething hatred due to the spikes of anger pumping through my veins.

"What the fuck does he see in you? What's with you black women anyway? It's not enough you're nabbing all the white men you have to come for the Italian men too?"

I shook my head. "I didn't—"

"Shut the fuck up and sit the fuck down!" she shouted, so loud her voice cracked.

As soon as my butt hit the smooth leather of the chair, the hard metal tip of her gun was at the base of my skull, pressing so hard it forced my head down.

"Do you know what I've endured to try and get his fucking attention? And as soon as I do, here you come, out of fucking-nowhere, but I'm about to fix that shit. You don't deserve him, and he can't move on because he's stuck on you. You with your melanin, kinky hair, and *phat* ass. I don't understand the appeal."

She said the words like she was spitting out phlegm. She shoved the pistol harder into the back of my head with each angry sentence she spat. My nerves were wracked with trembling fear waiting for the pop that would end my life. However, my curiosity didn't give a damn about my nerves. There were some questions I had to ask.

"Did you hire those men to kill Primo?"

Her silence answered before she did.

"Yes. But, if you know anything about Primo, it doesn't matter who you send, he'll find a way to end them."

"Why would you hire men if you knew he would kill them?"

This shit wasn't making one bit of sense.

"I had to make it look like I was in danger and needed him. Besides, I told the leader of the little crew I hired, who's dead now of course, to tell the rest of his men that it was a pretty black woman named Nevah who hired them. Primo caught the last two members a few days ago and if he tortures them like I know he will, they'll cracked, and guess who they are going to say hired them."

"No," I choked out. This bitch was stone crazy. She was going to put all this shit on me. My eyes darted around like marbles in my head while my brain worked overtime to first get out of this mess and second, find a way to prove to Primo that I didn't do any of this.

"Are you connected to the Vittorio family?" I finally asked her, remembering what Primo said about the Vittorio family possibly working with a DeLuca to kill him.

She released a low chuckle.

"Yes. I had to prove to them that I wasn't afraid to kill Primo. They hired contract killers. I had no idea the crazy fucks would hire a whole army. It didn't matter though, I expected Primo to kill everyone they sent after him. I wasn't too worried about him dying."

So, *she* was the reason for all these problems, deaths, and a potential war. All of this to win the heart of a man who didn't want her. What if he had died because of her? He still could die because of her. I closed my eyes and squeezed them into tight, trembling knots.

All the death and destruction I had witnessed in my younger years resurfaced and reminded me who I was. The memories of the time I'd had to take a life flared like fireworks in my brain and ignited my courage.

Leandra was gun brave. The false courage from holding that weapon kept her talking about the features she hated about me. While she was talking herself through the reasons why Primo wanted me, I was thinking up a way out of this position.

If she could manipulate another mob family to do her dirty work, this crazy ass bitch likely had Primo thinking I hired people to kill him. Why did she still feel threatened by me? The shit made no sense. *She* made no sense. No wonder Primo didn't want her.

I let my head fall to my chest before jerking it up and spun to get my hands under that gun. As suicidal as the move was, it worked. The gun went skyward, but she managed to hang on to it.

My little distraction gave me time to send another fist hard against her wrist, knocking the gun from her shaky grip. It flew to the left before gravity sucked it down to the marble floor with a hard, skittering thud.

Leandra stood in shock for a second before lunging for the weapon. I swiveled, fanning my leg out until the side of my foot connected and swept the weapon out of her reach.

Her tense jaw and set gaze met mine before her fist came at my head and missed. She was too slow, and I'd fought enough in the streets to know how to dodge a fist.

I drew my right leg up and into my body and kicked out. The stomping impact collided with her pelvic area and forced her to release a loud swish of air before she stumbled back.

"You fucking bitch!" she screamed, holding her mid-section and blowing out winded breaths. Based on the enraged glare glistening in her eyes, her anger had reached its boiling point, and she ran, charging towards me, releasing some sort of death cry.

My firm knee was waiting for her crazy ass and connected with her stomach so hard, the big gust of wind and spittle she released blasted against the side of my face. She was on the defense now. I remained relentless in my attack as she fought desperately to stop the blows I delivered to her head and shoulders.

I wasn't a hair-pulling, face scratching fighter. Instead, I learned from street brawlers to make every effort to hit them where it would hurt most. Take out their vision and their ability to breathe properly, and everything else they knew would be less effective.

Every once in a while, one of her wild punches and kicks connected with different parts of my body, but I didn't care. My adrenaline dulled the pain of her attack which allowed me to rain down punches on her.

She clawed until she got a good grip on my shirt and jerked, taking me down to the floor with her. Our bodies collided with the hard marble, her falling and landing on her ass, and my hip hitting the floor while the top half of me fell across her heaving chest.

We tussled, lobbing curse words, punches, and kicks for dominance. During our back-and-forth dance, she managed to climb atop me. I heaved and yelled to conjure up the strength needed to twist my body and lift, flipping and mounting her.

The gun came into view like a twinkling diamond in the sun, and she scrambled for it with me riding her back. The harsh pulls I gave her hair made her head jerk back viciously. Every attempt was meant to rip pieces of hair from her skull.

There was no calling each other bitches. Our shouts were primal and all about survival. This was a fight to the death. One of us was dying in this hotel room tonight.

I gasped, choking on the sharp breaths I was too winded to properly take. I poured all my strength into getting her bucking body under control while she continued reaching and dragging me along to get to the gun.

My flailing hands ended up wrapped around something hard and thick. I dragged the heavy item closer before lifting it and crashing it down over the top of her head. The blow slowed her down but didn't stop her, so I continued to crash what I discovered was the wooden bottom of one of the lamps into the side of her head.

Repeatedly, the loud *thumps* from the lamp base connecting with her head, vibrated into my hand, and echoed through my body. An unnatural *crack* registered before her skull caved. Blood coated the base, glistening like dark oil and making my hands slippery. I sent the lamp down a few more times, not stopping until she ceased all movement.

A loud breath of relief made a whistling sound when it flew from my mouth, thankful that she had stopped fighting. I rolled onto my back and remained that way beside her motionless body with my gaze pinned on the ceiling.

I breathed a loud chest-lifting cadence of huffs and puffs. A reluctant turn of my head put me face to face with her. The horrific sight spiked my already elevated heart rate. Wide, empty brown eyes met mine. Blood had splattered her makeup-smeared tan skin. Her mouth sat fixed and open, revealing her teeth painted pink and red with blood.

The natural rise and fall of her chest had frozen in its final moment. The emptiness that surrounded her sent an unnatural wave of knowing into me that caused my body to shiver. The blood pooling around her head and the sunken area at the top of her skull, indicated that I had cracked her cranium.

Leandra, a woman I saw sitting with Primo and spied on from the restaurant's restroom, was dead. The hand I was dealt this night was a losing one, almost mirroring how I'd had to fight off my husband all those years ago.

On the one hand, it was either her or me. On the other hand, the crazy bitch was a DeLuca. The worst possible hand would be Primo believing I hired assassins to kill him. He had revealed to me parts of his family history, including Leandra's identity. I also knew from common sense that killing a DeLuca came with a hefty price, like death.

I survived this crazy, scorned woman, but how was I going to survive the whole family when they came for me? How was I going to get myself out of this shit? I was still unsure how far her plot to make me out to be the bad guy had gone. Did Primo think Leandra the victim and me the facilitator of all this shit?

I believed Primo cared about me, but would it be enough if he believed I was involved in taking the life of multiple DeLucas and planning his assassination?

Chapter Twenty-five

Primo

Pride raced through me. Although my overall demeanor was usually set on "asshole," the men, for the most part, made my job as Capo an easy one. They pulled their weight, handled their business, and today they'd worked their asses off. With Aurelio's help, they managed to wrangle up the last of the hitmen hired by the Vittorio family who had foolishly taken on the task to take my life.

Three lay at our feet, their blood-drenched bodies in a heap while we discussed the best approach to improving our productivity and distribution efforts. Today was our normal meeting day, and despite the obvious need to expel our enemies, we had carved out some time to address business and operational concerns.

There was one problem we hadn't solved. We still didn't know how to kill the person who had initiated this blood-fueled quest to kill me for reasons we still weren't crystal clear on.

We discovered the identity of the DeLuca responsible for initiating the hit on me and the one responsible for the death of six of my men. The person was virtually untouchable based on our own rules. There were many suggestions and discussions on how to get away with the person's murder without breaking a cardinal DeLuca rule.

Poison and accidental death scenarios were tossed around, and even the idea of us setting up our own DeLuca prison. At the mention of a prison, Romigi glanced at me with a smile in his gaze.

Orlando's suggestion about distribution techniques dragged me back to the current topic of discussion. I shrugged when he kept his eyes on me, waiting for a response.

"I don't believe we need to add any additional hands or man-hours to our operations. If we include one more rotation versus our usual three, it may work to our benefit."

The elongated squeak of the front door sounded before it popped open. The unexpected use of that particular door caused weapons to be drawn. We usually entered through the side or back doors, and only the company we invited used the front door.

My face tightened into a ball of concern when Nevah came stumbling through the door. Her clothing was disheveled, discernible bruises decorated her neck and arms, and her normally well-maintained hair sprung up from multiple areas and fell from her high ponytail like she'd been inside a wind tunnel. I was at her side so fast I couldn't even recall how I got there.

"What happened?" I questioned, holding her shoulders while her wild-eyed glance met my searching gaze with a glint in their untamed depths I couldn't decipher. She smelled like she'd bathed in bleach and I didn't miss that she'd flinched at my touch.

"Are we still good? Me and you?"

I nodded.

"We were never bad. Is everything alright? What happened to you?"

"Good," she replied before she blew out a big breath of relief.

She aimed a finger at my guys, most standing in wide-eyed anticipation and no doubt wondering why the only woman I publicly claimed had shown up here. This was the second DeLuca meeting that Nevah had crashed, and like the first time, the men were expecting an explanation.

"Can I talk to everyone? I have a confession I need to make before I lose my nerve and change my mind."

Lowering my tone, I asked, "What kind of confession?"

She didn't answer but returned a look of defiance, or was it determination?

I eased back, putting space between us. I already felt bad about sending Aurelio to question her. But, he had put my mind at ease and had even given me a compliment for finding a good woman.

My aim now was to respect Nevah and there was no better way to do that than to start with honoring her current request. I ushered my hand towards the men to open the floor for her to address them.

The act of me allowing her to speak would make a statement I didn't like, but I forced myself to accept a truth I was skirting. She was the only force in my life that I couldn't command in the ways that I was used to. Besides, she hadn't asked for this life, and whatever fresh hell she had been through tonight was assuredly brought on in the name of DeLuca.

She smoothed her hair down and straightened her clothing as best she could before she sucked in a deep, shaky breath that closed her eyes. She stepped away and approached the group of fifteen, who gave their undivided attention.

"I know you guys don't know me well. Some of you have only seen my face a few times. I'm a stranger, an outsider, but I know the codes of the streets. I know them well because I grew up in *The Grind,* in the Sunset Heights housing projects."

The guys peered at each other with multiple levels of interest, some with their eyebrows lifting high on their foreheads. They were just now realizing what I picked up on the first time I met Nevah. Her statement regarding her background was enough to prove that she wasn't a distressed damsel but a woman raised in an environment that matched our inherently savage nature.

"The streets raised me, and they didn't take it easy on me because I was a girl. They insisted on me being smart, loyal, honest, and strong." She paused, swallowing and gathering her thoughts. "Tonight, when I stepped into my hotel suite, there was someone there waiting for me. That person threatened my life with a gun. They wanted me dead so that they could get to Primo."

She placed her hand over her heart. Tears glistened in her eyes but didn't fall.

"I love him, and I couldn't let that happen. I couldn't give that person what they wanted."

All of the sound was sucked from the room. The constant noises of machines being operated from surrounding warehouses that usually seeped into ours had stopped. The slush of the river crashing against the dock was silenced. Even the whistling wind that howled at the old dusty windows high on the walls surrounding the warehouse had stopped.

I, for the first time in my life, was tongue-tied and stood anchored in my shock while Nevah turned towards the front door and took shaky steps away. My lips parted, but words continued to escape me, lost in the energy of the three words she had just unleashed on me and my family.

After a confession like that, the men stood in place with their faces etched in deep, confusing frowns, not only for her endearing declaration, but for what sounded like a deadly confession that followed.

We had just spent hours before our business meeting trying to figure out how to kill our DeLuca rat, a rat that some of the men suspected was Nevah. Now, her confession had them mentally exhausted.

They remained silent, not knowing what to make of Nevah's cryptic confession or how to react to her because of me. It sounded like she'd had to kill to defend me, which meant defending the family.

However, I read the questions mounting in the tight set of shoulders and in the squints of the looks being exchanged.

Did she kill someone?
Who had she killed?

Three men were assigned to watch Nevah, so I had a few questions of my own. How had someone found her? How had they gotten to her? Was it another of the hitmen? How had she ended up coming face to face with a situation that she believed she needed to reveal to us in this manner?

As if a moment of clarity hit her, Nevah turned back to the group. She aimed a finger at the door.

"I'm going to get the body."

The men looked to me for answers when she disappeared from sight. I shrugged before lifting my hands. Every instinct within me wanted to go after her. However, I got the sense that she wanted to do this her way, so I was going to let her.

The door snapped open again, and she propped it open with the splintering doorstop that sat near it. She disappeared from sight once more and returned, dragging a large black suitcase. The weight of the body inside had her winded and pulling it with cautious back steps. She stopped and dropped the suitcase in front of our half circle.

We waited with our eyes locked on the suitcase before our gazes shot to Nevah. We hadn't had this much intrigue occur among us in a long time. Brizio gave me an expression that posed the question, *Who's in the suitcase?*

Nevah stooped and reached for the zipper while glancing up at all of us.

"I knew it would be a fight to the death the moment I found this person inside my room. I know that I should be sorry for taking a life, but I'm not sorry for taking a life to defend my own."

I hadn't experienced this much tension, not even when I was preparing to complete my first mission at eighteen for the Don.

Nevah unzipped the luggage, and although there was a crack that allowed a peek into it, we only saw a glimpse of dark denim material. She placed her hand on either side of the top cover, preparing to spring it open.

"This person. They are DeLuca."

The collective gasps and sighs were released into the space like a toxic cloud had burst and set free its poison. Not a word was uttered. Not a muscle was moved, not even a twitch until all eyes landed on me—again.

My fucking inner voice was screaming in five different tones, representing the emotions I was experiencing. Guilt, anger, and regret were the major three. I had dragged Nevah into this situation.

Instead of being intimidated by what she must have known would land her in trouble with the family, she stared each man in the eye. The situation had stunned them into unmoving mannequins, a feat I wasn't sure I could have accomplished with the group. Despite what they may have felt about the death of another DeLuca, intrigue rested heavily on their faces. They wanted to see that body.

When Nevah flipped the top of the luggage open, our heads tilted first, and our bodies followed, angling for a closer view. Eyes started squinting, and a few even took a step or two closer with their gazes laser-locked on the body that was bent like that of a contortionist.

Nevah stood tall, aiming a finger at the body. "She admitted that she was obsessed with Primo and would kill me to get to him. She was the one who hired those men to kill Primo. I know it sounds crazy, but it's true."

She breathed through her anxiety before continuing.

"But tonight it was either her or me. I understand that in this family, killing a Deluca..."

She swallowed hard. The little tremble in her bottom lip expressed her sorrow. When her eyes landed on the big grin on my face, her brows pinched at my expression. She tore her gaze away from mine to scan the room. Her eyes roamed restlessly and gradually widened at the sight of all the smiles forming.

"You need to marry her to-fucking-day, Primo!" Brizio yelled out.

Words of agreement from the rest of the group followed his statement.

"I'm ordained. I can marry you two right now," Romigi announced, confusing Nevah even further.

I approached her, hoping my expression beamed with the pride and gratefulness I felt for having such a fierce and beautiful woman in my life.

Ever since Franco informed me about her background, specifically the news about her having to kill her husband for beating her on multiple occasions, I was certain that she would eventually settle into the DeLuca family.

Without hesitation, I walked up to her, wrapped my arms around her, and lifted her up off her feet. In the background, the men cheered, hooted, and howled. Nevah was stiff in my arms, with her face pinched in a tight knot of confusion.

"You are amazing. You know that. And I love you too," I said before placing my lips against her parted ones. She didn't fight the kiss but allowed her lips to melt into mine until the flaming heat we produced together forced us to devour each other.

By the time I turned Nevah loose, the cheers had grown louder with claps and shouts so rowdy, the vibrations rattled my insides. I took Nevah's face between my palms.

"We've been trying to figure out how to kill Leandra for a few days now, unable to touch her because of one of our cardinal rules."

"Oh," she said, letting a small smile rest on her lips. She aimed a finger at the suitcase, but her words seemed to be hung up in her throat, so I started up again.

"*She* was the DeLuca who hired those hitmen to take me out. She was obsessed, but I'm not convinced it was necessarily with me. I believe she was more obsessed with the position of power I represented. You remember, I told you she was married to my cousin, Emmanuelle, who was the Capo before me?"

Her head fell slowly into an uncertain nod.

"When he threatened her with divorce, she killed him and had one of her cousins help her cover it up."

Based on Nevah's tight brows, I was adding to her confusion.

"A few days ago, we found out that before Leandra became a DeLuca, she was a Vittorio by marriage. She went by her maiden name, Espisito, so we were none the wiser that Emmanuelle had married the enemy. We believe she infiltrated our family as a spy for her family."

"Wow," was Nevah's response.

"Leandra found out quickly that the DeLuca name meant power. Somewhere along the way, we think one of two things happened. One: she lost sight of what she had infiltrated our family for and focused her obsession on the residual power she possessed being married to a DeLuca man. After she'd had to kill Emmanuelle, she set her sights on me next. When she discovered that I wasn't interested, she was willing to take me out to get her hands on the next in line and the next after that if it came to it."

"Damn," Nevah huffed out, her wide gaze expressing disbelief. "You said one of two things happened. What's the second?"

"Humbling our egos. It may not have been about her obsession with the DeLuca men or power at all. We believe she was under pressure by her family to stir up chaos at a vulnerable time for our family, which should have allowed the Vittorios a chance to swoop in and take control of some of our operations.

"We believe they tried the same thing after she killed Emmanuelle, but their efforts weren't strong enough to accomplish the failed attempts they launched at us. We killed three Vittorios after Emmanuelle's death, unaware that the incidents were connected to Leandra."

Nevah shook her head, her thoughts racing.

"The way she was talking in that hotel room, it sounded like she was counting on you taking out her family, so she would be free to be with you. She also hired some men to make it look like she was the victim, even telling them to tell you that I hired them if they were ever caught."

My head shook at her update, since we had pieced together most of Leandra's deception. All I could think was what if I didn't follow my gut and believed the lies of a mad woman over the truth that resided in my heart.

"What happens now? She's a member of a family who wants you dead. Will there be war?" she questioned, glancing down at Leandra's body.

"I doubt it. The Vittorios have crossed too many lines and have suffered too many big losses to be foolish enough to come at us. If they had anything we truly wanted, it would be the perfect time for us to attack them."

She paused, taking in her surroundings with a roving eye before her gaze met mine again. Relief was what I read in her observant eyes.

"You don't have any more women out there that are willing to kill and start wars to get your attention, do you?"

"No. But, even if I did, I have you to take care of them."

She shook her head before a crooked smile graced her sexy lips.

Epilogue

Nevah

A month later.

"Aww! Oh baby! Don't you dare stop!"

My shrieking cries, moans, yells, and whatever else decided to fly out of my mouth had the sea life in my immediate view scurrying away. I caught the quick flicks of their tails and fins zooming through the beautiful crystal blue water every time Primo hit a spot that had me begging and pleading for more and for him to go harder and deeper.

We were putting the overwater bungalow we stayed in to good use. Bent over the fancy guardrail, we made excellent use of our private balcony. If some far off boat or ship happened to see us, they may have been inclined to call the authorities, thinking I needed to be rescued from the savage beating this man was putting on my pussy.

The harder he fuck me, the better it seemed to feel. Primo was the only man that could get me to a point of no return during sex. We were at that point now, so uninhibited and ravenous that we were putting wild animals to shame.

Breathless and giving my vocal cords as much of a workout as my body, I yelled, moaned, and cried through my release.

"Primo! Yes baby. Make. Me. Come. All. Over. Over."

Who the hell knew what I was trying to say? I damn well didn't. My fractured words didn't matter because I was in a state of heavenly bliss, our sex a drug we dosed ourselves in every chance we got.

***

The next day.

The rays of the sun brushed warmth against my skin, the breeze tickling along the surface, while the ocean hummed a melody. The three teamed up to produce the perfect mix for relaxation.

A deep inhale lifted my chest high before I released it with ease. My face was aimed at the sky while I lay stretched out on a beach chair. A shadow broke the warmth of the rays I enjoyed, and an instant smile dashed across my lips at the sight of who blocked the sun.

"Here's your drink, Mrs. DeLuca."

"Thank you, Mr. DeLuca."

"I can't believe I let you talk me into taking a honeymoon," he said, glancing around and taking in the beautiful beach scenery. "However, I have to admit that this first-time experience is one I'm enjoying. Who knew how much fun it could be to do nothing but sit on my ass, eat, and drink? And the things we do in private are tempting me to extend our stay by a week."

"Told you you'd have a good time."

Primo sipped his rum punch and sat back on his lounge chair. We blended into the crowd of normal couples. There were no hitmen, obsessed want-to-be girlfriends, car chases, or any number of dangerous situations that I agreed to when I said "I do" to Primo a week ago. We had crashed another family meeting so that his cousin, Romigi, could marry us.

"What does a DeLuca wife do?" I glanced at my husband with one brow lifted.

"I can't speak for other DeLuca wives, but mine will do whatever the hell she wants."

My smile grew to about a mile wide. "All I want is to be the best nurse I can be, support and make my husband happy, and live our best lives."

The statement had him grinning now. He leaned over my chair, placing a peck first on my forehead, my cheek, and then my lips. "Are you ready to return to that magical bungalow you booked?"

The lust in his eyes revealed what he wanted, and I was happy to oblige, nodding before he could finish asking the question.

"My wife said she wants to make me happy, and with the way we've been fucking, it looks like I'm going to have a son or daughter before my old ass turns forty."

I shook my head, unable to hold in my outburst of laughter. Truth be told, I was praying he knocked me up before we left this island. His behavior and his treatment of me had never wavered. I had dated straight-laced and criminal, blue-collar and white-collar workers, and none had ever made me feel like the most precious thing in their lives.

Primo was unquestionably the man for me.

We walked hand and hand towards our suite, my head resting against his sturdy shoulder. The sand pushed its way between my toes, adding to the feeling of contentment that my husband never failed to fill me with.

Happiness was something that had eluded me with men in the past, to the point that I gave up on love. Who knew that I would find genuine happiness with a DeLuca savage named Primo?

End of Primo DeLuca

Acknowledgment

USA Today Best Selling Author was an achievement I accomplished with a group of Savage Authors I admire and respect. I would like to extend a special Thank You to Author Siren Allen and Author Shani Greene-Dowell. I'm eternally grateful to you for spearheading this mission and inviting me to join the team.

Thanks to all of the Savage Bloodline Authors who made working on this dream team one of the easiest and enjoyable experiences of my writing career.

Thank you to the fierce readers who supported and still continue to support this savage bloodline collection. You are the best motivation any author could ever hope for and my appreciation for you is immeasurable.

Author's Note

Readers, my sincere thank you for reading Primo DeLuca. I appreciate your time and every page flipped. Please leave a review or star rating letting me and others know what you thought of this Savage DeLuca Alpha and his lady Nevah. If you enjoyed it or any of my other books, please pass them along to friends or anyone you think would enjoy them.

Other Titles by Keta Kendric

The Twisted Minds Series:

Twisted Minds #1
Twisted Hearts #2
Twisted Secrets #3
Twisted Obsession #4
Twisted Revelation #5
Twisted Deception # 6 (2024)

The Chaos Series:

Beautiful Chaos #1
Quiet Chaos #2

<u>Hidden Chaos#3</u>

Stand Alones:

<u>Severe</u>

<u>Roots of the Wicked</u>

Brizio DeLuca

Novellas:

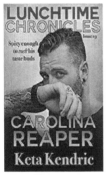

Carolina Reaper

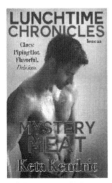

Mystery Meat

Spice Cake

Contemporary Series:

Love Lied Series

Paranormals:

Sevyn

Smoke

The Box

Kindle Vella:

Love Lied Series

Audiobooks:

Connect on Social Media

Subscribe to my Newsletter or Paranormal Newsletter for exclusive updates on new releases, sneak peeks, and much more.

You can also follow me on:

Newsletter Sign up: https://mailchi.mp/c5ed185fd868/httpsmailchimp

Paranormal Newsletter Sign up: https://mailchi.mp/38b87cb6232d/keta-kendric-paranormal-newsletter

Instagram: https://instagram.com/ketakendric

Facebook Readers' Group: https://www.face-book.com/groups/380642765697205/

BookBub: https://www.bookbub.com/authors/keta-kendric

Twitter: https://twitter.com/AuthorKetaK

Goodreads: https://www.goodreads.com/user/show/73387641-keta-kendric

TikTok: https://www.tiktok.com/@ketakendric?

Pinterest: https://www.pinterest.com/authorslist/

Made in the USA
Middletown, DE
05 November 2024

63564214R00170